'Hilarious and cracklingly intelligent, fully alive and original in every sentence' Jonathan Franzen

'I was both amused and appalled by the anti-hero of Ben Lerner's *Leaving the Atocha Station*' David Nicholls, *Guardian* Books of the Year

'Short but potent . . . Lerner sets up profound questions about the possibilities of art and human experience' *The Times*

'Hugely entertaining' Liz Jensen, BBC Radio 4 *Saturday Review*

'Lerner makes a kind of refined comedy out of his grad student narrator's gnawing sense of his own inauthenticity' *New Statesman* Books of the Year

'One of the most exciting aspects of *Leaving the Atocha Station* is seeing a dedicated poet write a novel that addresses poetry's limitations . . . One half-wonders if, in the future, this model will loom as large in the minds of young artists as the Romantics and the modernists do in ours' Sheila Heti, *London Review of Books*

'Comic [but] also beautiful and touching and precise' *Guardian*

'Beautifully written . . . An anatomy of a generation's uncertainty and self-involvement, *Leaving the Atocha Station* offers a carefully constructed snapshot of a nation in doubt, torn in different directions, while its narrator – like everyone else – tries to "dwell among contradictions"' *Times Literary Supplement*

'Wonderful precision and comic timing . . . Superb' *Metro*

'It made me laugh so much . . . I thought it was brilliant. I loved it right to the last page' Paul Farley, BBC Radio 4 *Saturday Review*

'A ma

Leaving the Atocha Station

A NOVEL

BEN LERNER

GRANTA

Granta Publications, 12 Addison Avenue, London W11 4QR

First published in Great Britain by Granta Books 2012
Paperback edition published by Granta Books 2013
Originally published in the United States by Coffee House Press,
Minneapolis 2011

A CIP catalogue record for this book is available from the British Library.

9 10 8

ISBN 978 1 84708 691 4

Offset by Avon DataSet Ltd, Bidford on Avon, Warwickshire

Printed and bound by CPI Group (UK) Ltd, Croydon, CR0 4YY

MIX
Paper from
responsible sources
FSC® C020471

1

THE FIRST PHASE OF MY RESEARCH INVOLVED WAKING UP WEEKDAY mornings in a barely furnished attic apartment, the first apartment I'd looked at after arriving in Madrid, or letting myself be woken by the noise from La Plaza Santa Ana, failing to assimilate that noise fully into my dream, then putting on the rusty stovetop espresso machine and rolling a spliff while I waited for the coffee. When the coffee was ready I would open the skylight, which was just big enough for me to crawl through if I stood on the bed, and drink my espresso and smoke on the roof overlooking the plaza where tourists congregated with their guidebooks on the metal tables and the accordion player plied his trade. In the distance: the palace and long lines of cloud. Next my project required dropping myself back through the skylight, shitting, taking a shower, my white pills, and getting dressed. Then I'd find my bag, which contained a bilingual edition of Lorca's *Collected Poems,* my two notebooks, a pocket dictionary, John Ashbery's *Selected Poems,* drugs, and leave for the Prado.

From my apartment I would walk down Calle de las Huertas, nodding to the street cleaners in their lime-green jumpsuits, cross El Paseo del Prado, enter the museum, which was only a couple of euros with my international student ID, and proceed directly to room 58, where I positioned myself in front of Roger Van der

Weyden's *Descent from the Cross*. I was usually standing before the painting within forty-five minutes of waking and so the hash and caffeine and sleep were still competing in my system as I faced the nearly life-sized figures and awaited equilibrium. Mary is forever falling to the ground in a faint; the blues of her robes are unsurpassed in Flemish painting. Her posture is almost an exact echo of Jesus's; Nicodemus and a helper hold his apparently weightless body in the air. C.1435; 220 x 262 cm. Oil on oak paneling.

A turning point in my project: I arrived one morning at the Van der Weyden to find someone had taken my place. He was standing exactly where I normally stood and for a moment I was startled, as if beholding myself beholding the painting, although he was thinner and darker than I. I waited for him to move on, but he didn't. I wondered if he had observed me in front of the *Descent* and if he was now standing before it in the hope of seeing whatever it was I must have seen. I was irritated and tried to find another canvas for my morning ritual, but was too accustomed to the painting's dimensions and blues to accept a substitute. I was about to abandon room 58 when the man broke suddenly into tears, convulsively catching his breath. Was he, I wondered, just facing the wall to hide his face as he dealt with whatever grief he'd brought into the museum? Or was he having a *profound experience of art*?

I had long worried that I was incapable of having a profound experience of art and I had trouble believing that anyone had, at least anyone I knew. I was intensely suspicious of people who claimed a poem or painting or piece of music "changed their life," especially since I had often known these people before and after their experience and could register no change. Although I claimed to be a poet, although my supposed talent as a writer had earned me my fellowship in Spain, I tended to find lines of poetry beautiful only when I encountered them quoted in prose, in the essays my professors had assigned in college, where the line breaks were replaced with slashes, so that what was communicated was less a particular poem than the echo of poetic possibility. Insofar as I was interested in the arts, I was interested in the disconnect between my experience of actual artworks and the claims made on their behalf; the closest I'd come to having a profound experience of art was probably the experience of this distance, a profound experience of the absence of profundity.

Once the man calmed down, which took at least two minutes, he wiped his face and blew his nose with a handkerchief he then returned to his pocket. On entering room 57, which was empty except for a lanky and sleepy guard, the man walked immediately up to the small votive image of Christ attributed to San Leocadio: green tunic, red robes, expression of deep sorrow. I pretended to take in other paintings while looking sidelong at the man as he considered the little canvas. For a long minute he was quiet and then he again released a sob. This startled the guard into alertness and our eyes met, mine saying that this had happened in the other gallery, the guard's communicating his struggle to determine whether the man was crazy—perhaps the kind of man who would damage a painting, spit on it or tear it from the wall or scratch it with a key— or if the man was having a profound experience of art. Out came the handkerchief and the man walked calmly into 56, stood before *The Garden of Earthly Delights,* considered it calmly, then totally lost his shit. Now there were three guards in the room—the lanky guard from 57, the short woman who always guarded 56, and an older guard with improbably long silver hair who must have heard the most recent outburst from the hall. The one or two other museum-goers in 56 were deep in their audio tours and oblivious to the scene unfolding before the Bosch.

What is a museum guard to do, I thought to myself; what, really, *is* a museum guard? On the one hand you are a member of a security force charged with protecting priceless materials from the crazed or kids or the slow erosive force of camera flashes; on the other hand you are a dweller among supposed triumphs of the spirit and if your position has any prestige it derives precisely from the belief that such triumphs could legitimately move a man to tears. There was a certain pathos in the indecision of the guards, guards who spend much of their lives in front of timeless paintings but are only ever asked what time is it, when does the museum close, dónde esta el baño. I could not share the man's rapture, if that's what it was, but I found myself moved by the dilemma of the guards: should they ask the man to step into the hall and attempt to ascertain his mental state, no doubt ruining his profound experience, or should they risk letting this potential lunatic loose among the treasures of their culture, no doubt risking, among other things, their jobs? I found their mute performance of these tensions more moving than any *Pietà, Deposition,* or *Annunciation,* and I felt like one of their company as we trailed the man from gallery to gallery. Maybe this man is an artist, I thought; what if he doesn't feel the transports he performs, what if the scenes he produces are intended to force the institution to face its contradiction in the person of these guards. I was thinking something like this as the man concluded another fit of weeping and headed calmly for the museum's main exit. The guards disbanded with, it seemed to me, less relief than sadness, and I found myself following this man, this great artist, out of the museum and into the preternaturally bright day.

———

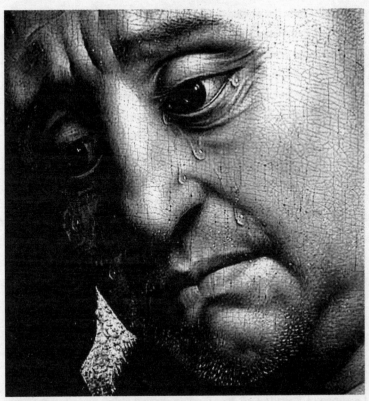

I thought of the great artist for a while.

Most weekends during the first phase of my research, my Spanish tutor, Jorge, whom the foundation paid to help its fellows move rapidly from proficiency to fluency, would drive me to a campsite forty minutes outside of Madrid where his friends from the language school went to get high and drink, swim, hook up. They called me El Poeta, whether with derision or affection I never really learned. I bought most of the beer and I was also buying my hash from Jorge, who radically overcharged. The campground itself was nothing to speak of: a clearing with a couple of fire pits, a fair amount of litter, although I never saw anyone near the site except for us, and we were careful to clean up. It was less than a hundred feet to the lake. It was usually warm enough to sleep outside. Few words were addressed to me when the five or six of us were sitting around the fire drinking and smoking my hash or the powerful weed Jorge introduced as it got late. I almost never spoke, although I tried to smile, and to imply with my smile that I understood what was being said around me, letting it fluctuate as though in reaction to their speech.

One night when I was particularly high, I gradually realized Jorge was saying my name, not Poeta, saying it sharply, and the others were looking at me with anger, disbelief. Then I realized that I had been smiling my smile, just holding it there, paying no attention, while one of Jorge's friends, Isabel, was telling what must have been a tragic story or confessing something painful, at least her voice was quiet and her tears were catching firelight. It took me what felt like a minute to work my face out of the smile, a smile they thought was my response to Isabel's plight. On this rare occasion I decided to attempt speech: I didn't understand, I tried to say, or I didn't listen, but whatever I stammered was unintelligible, barely Spanish. All I needed to say was that I'd zoned out, drifted off, was terribly sorry if Isabel had thought I was smiling at her story, but I couldn't think of how to say this or any other thing. Worse, the smile came back automatically as I guessed they were telling me how fucked up it was to react to whatever Isabel was describing in this way. Then Jorge's friend Miguel, who was either related to or enamored with Isabel, threw his can of beer at me from across the fire and told me to wipe that smile off my face, if they have that expression in Spain. I laughed involuntarily, nervously, except that to my horror my laugh didn't sound nervous, compounding the insult to Isabel, whose head was now in her hands. Isabel rose, left the fire, and headed for the lake, followed by the other two women in our group, while Miguel approached and stood over me threatening something; Jorge held him back. I was at least by this time repeating I'm sorry, I'm sorry, but Miguel broke loose or Jorge released him and he hit me in the mouth.

It wasn't a powerful blow, but I figured I should let it lay me out. Miguel was screaming at me and the noise brought Isabel and her friends back from the lake. Miguel allowed Jorge to pull him away and calm him down. I could taste the blood from my mildly cut lip and I bit hard to deepen the cut so that I would appear more injured and therefore solicit sufficient sympathy to offset the damage my smiling had done. As I covered my face in my hands and writhed as though in pain, I was careful to spread the blood around, and when I picked myself up and reentered the firelight Isabel gasped and said my mother, my God. I walked out of the ensuing silence down to the lake and began to wash my face. After a few minutes I heard footsteps on the dry grass: Isabel.

"I'm sorry," she said.

"No, I'm sorry," I said. "I don't understand what story you said before to me," is probably what I said. "My Spanish is very bad. I get nervous."

"Your Spanish is good," she said. "How is your face?"

"My face is good," I said, which made her laugh. She undid her hair and took the scarf and dipped it and wrung it out and used it to wipe the rest of the blood from my face and then dipped it and wrung it out. She began to say something either about the moon, the effect of the moon on the water, or was using the full moon to excuse Miguel or the evening's general drama, though the moon wasn't full. Her hair was long, maybe longer than the guard's. Then she might have described swimming in the lake as a child, or said that lakes reminded her of being a child, or asked me if I'd enjoyed swimming as a child, or said that what she'd said about the moon was childish. She asked me if I knew a poem by Lorca, this time about something that involved several colors and required her to softly roll her *r*'s, which I couldn't do. She offered me a cigarette and we smoked and I looked at the water and was sober.

I wanted to know what she had been crying about and I managed to communicate that desire mainly by repeating the words for "fire" and "before." She paused for a long moment and then began to speak; something about a home, but whether she meant a household or the literal structure, I couldn't tell; I heard the names of streets and months; a list of things I thought were books or songs; hard times or hard weather, epoch, uncle, change, an analogy involving summer, something about buying and/or crashing a red car. I formed several possible stories out of her speech, formed them at once, so it was less like I failed to understand than that I understood in chords, understood in a plurality of worlds. Her uncle had died in a car crash a year ago today in a street in Salamanca; she had helped have her junky boyfriend hospitalized over the summer and now he wouldn't see her and had moved to Barcelona; her parents, who lived in a small town, were having their home foreclosed upon and she had been sorting through boxes of childhood toys; she had broken with a sibling over the war. This ability to dwell among possible referents, to let them interfere and separate like waves, to abandon the law of excluded middle while listening to Spanish— this was a breakthrough in my project, a change of phase. I kept quiet, modeling my face on the San Leocadio.

———

From the Prado I would typically walk to a small café called El Rincón where I'd eat a sandwich, just hard bread and chorizo, and where I would be the only person eating, unless there were tourists, since it wasn't close to lunchtime for the Spanish. Then I'd walk a few blocks more to El Retiro, the city's central park, find a bench, take out my notebooks, the pocket dictionary, Lorca, and get high.

If the sun were out and I proportioned the hash and tobacco correctly, if there were other people around, but at a distance, so that I could hear that they were speaking without hearing in which language, a small wave of euphoria would break over me. There were hours and hours of light left, for the Spanish it wasn't even really afternoon; there were months and months of my fellowship left, it had only just begun; but the fellowship wouldn't go on too long— I would be returned to my life at such and such a date, a little more interesting to everyone for my time abroad, thinner probably, otherwise unchanged. I didn't need to establish a life in Madrid beyond the simplest routines; I didn't have to worry about building a community, whatever that meant. I had the endless day, months and months of endless days, and yet my return date bounded this sense of boundlessness, kept it from becoming threatening. I would begin to feel a rush of what I considered love, first for the things at hand: the swifts, if that's what they were, hopping in the dust, the avenues of old-world trees, the stone statues of kings and queens with whom the tourists pose, love for the glare off El Estanque, the park's artificial lake. Love for Topeka: the chicken hawk atop the telephone poll, the man-child with a flare gun tucked into his sweatpants, the finger lost to snapping turtle or firework; love for the bully and his neck beard, a love only a mother could face. Love for all my sitters, except James; love for the wrestler falling from the water tower where he'd tried to represent. Then for Providence: the first breakdown in the stacks, running lines of prescription something with the dim kids of the stars, emerging from a tunnel or sleep into New York, redefining "rich," love for the unread book of poems, Cyrus and our walks. But most intensely love for *that other thing,* the sound-absorbent screen, life's white machine, shadows massing in the middle distance, although that's not even close, the texture of et cetera itself.

On these days I worked on what I called translation. I opened the Lorca more or less at random, transcribed the English recto onto a page of my first notebook, and began to make changes, replacing a word with whatever word I first associated with it and/or scrambling the order of the lines, and then I made whatever changes these changes suggested to me. Or I looked up the Spanish word for the English word I wanted to replace, and then replaced that word with an English word that approximated its sound ("Under the arc of the sky" became "Under the arc of the cielo," which became "Under the arc of the cello"). I then braided fragments of the prose I kept in my second notebook with the translations I had thus produced ("Under the arc of the cello / I open the Lorca at random," and so on).

But if there were no sun and the proportioning was off, if there were either too many people around or if the park was empty, an abyss opened up inside me as I smoked. Now the afternoon was boundless in a terrifying way; it would never be tonight or the next day in room 58; silver and green drained from the landscape. I couldn't bring myself to open the book. It was worse than having a sinking feeling; I *was* a sinking feeling, an unplayable adagio for strings; internal distances expanded and collapsed when I breathed. It was like failing to have awoken at the right point in a nightmare; now you had to live in it, make yourself at home. He, if I can put it that way, had felt this as a child when they sent him to camp; his heart seemed at once to race and stop. Then his breath caught, flattened, shattered; as though a window had broken at thirty thousand feet, there was a sudden vacuum. Some of the gray was sucked inside him, and he was at a loss; he became a symptom of himself. He summoned the strength to reach into his bag, open the childproof bottle, touch the yellow pill to his tongue, crush it between his index finger and his thumb, and return its moist remains to the floor of his mouth. Then he waited and waited and finally the edge of something dulled. He became aware that he was warm; no, aware he had been cold. He touched his hands to his face and found both alien; the former were still freezing, the latter getting hot. He thought of the pay phones beside El Estanque; he could use his calling card; he could have someone at home talk him down. But it was seven or eight hours earlier there, everyone was sleeping. And what kind of grown man, if that's what he was, calls home in a panic for no definable reason, as he had called home from camp as a child, sobbing, please come pick me up. He became aware of a strange taste in his mouth; his saliva belonged to someone else; it made him sick to swallow. This, he said to himself with authority, is a sign of schizophrenia; this is the beginning of the rapid fragmentation of your so-called personality; you will have to be hospitalized. He could feel the paper gown against his skin. He crushed a second tranquilizer and stood up, legs barely his, and began walking toward the main gates. The other pedestrians on El Paseo del Prado regarded him strangely; he had the distinct sense that each person stopped as he passed and turned to watch; it was difficult not to run; his apartment receded at his approach; laughter issued from each passing car. Knowing none of it was real only made it that much worse.

He would rush up the six flights of stairs, find the key, drop the bag, and throw himself on the bed. He would cover himself entirely with the blanket. He would take my siesta then.

———

Most days when I awoke from my siesta, I put on the stovetop espresso machine, rolling a spliff while I waited for the coffee. When it was ready I turned on the shower and when the water was hot I stepped into the shower and took my coffee there, letting the water dilute the espresso as I drank it, letting the steam and caffeine slowly clear my head.

During the first phase of my research, I thought all Madrid slept during the siesta, and I drifted off imagining I was joining the rest of the slumbering capital, although later I learned that, of all the people I knew in Madrid, I was the only person who actually used this time to sleep. Whether my translation had gone well in El Retiro or whether I had sucked the grayness into my chest, I almost always felt the same after the siesta, that is, I felt nothing, although I would sleep for an extra hour if I had taken the tranqs, and if I'd been particularly upset, there was something like a faint chemical sting in the back of my mouth. I had known this chemical sting since I was a child and had assumed everyone knew it, that it was at least as universal as the coppery taste of blood, and somehow related, although later I learned that nobody I knew was familiar with this taste, at least not as I described it, not as the particular aftertaste of panic. I had never napped at home and the siesta had a dramatic effect on my sense of time, either seeming to double the day, so that remembering the morning was like remembering something on the other side of night, or supplanting the first half of the day entirely.

When I had dried myself off and dressed, I lit the spliff, poured the rest of the espresso and, if I'd finished a translation in the park, typed it up on my laptop and e-mailed it to Cyrus. Although I had internet access in my apartment, I claimed in my e-mails to be writing from an internet café and that my time was very limited. I tried my best not to respond to most of the e-mails I received as I thought this would create the impression I was offline, busy accumulating experience, while in fact I spent a good amount of time online, especially in the late afternoon and early evening, looking at videos of terrible things. After writing Cyrus, I would attempt to read the Quixote in a bilingual edition, eat something, usually chorizo, hard cheese, olives, and white asparagus from a jar, open a bottle of wine, abandon the Quixote and read Tolstoy in English; his major novels had been remaindered at Casa del Libro.

My plan had been to teach myself Spanish by reading masterworks of Spanish literature and I had fantasized about the nature and effect of a Spanish thus learned, how its archaic flavor and formally heightened rhetoric would collide with the mundanities of daily life, giving the impression less of someone from a foreign country than someone from a foreign time; I imagined using a beautiful and rarefied turn of phrase around the campfire after Jorge had broken out the powerful weed and watching the faces of the others as they realized their failure to understand me was not the issue of my ignorance or accent but their own remove from the zenith of their language. I imagined myself from their perspective once I'd obtained fluency in this elevated idiom: auratic, my example coming to stand for some dormant power within their own language, so that henceforth even my silences would seem well wrought, eloquent. But I couldn't bring myself to work at prose in Spanish, in part because I had to look up so many words that I was never able to experience the motion of a sentence; it remained so many particles, never a wave; I didn't have the patience to reread the same passage again and again until the words ceased to be mere points and formed a line. I came to realize that far more important to me than any plot or conventional sense was the sheer directionality I felt while reading prose, the texture of time as it passed, life's white machine. Even in the most dramatic scenes, when Natasha is suddenly beside him or whatever, what moved me most was less the pathos of the reunion and his passing than the action of prepositions, conjunctions, etc.; the sweep of predication was more compelling than the predicated.

Reading poetry, if reading is even the word, was something else entirely. Poetry actively repelled my attention, it was opaque and thingly and refused to absorb me; its articles and conjunctions and prepositions failed to dissolve into a feeling and a speed; you could fall into the spaces between words as you tried to link them up; and yet by refusing to absorb me the poem held out the possibility of a higher form of absorption of which I was unworthy, a profound experience unavailable from within the damaged life, and so the poem became a figure for its outside. It was much easier for me to read a poem in Spanish than Spanish prose because all the unknowing and hesitation and failure involved in the attempt to experience the poem was familiar, it was what invested any poem with a negative power, its failure to move me moved me, at least a little; my inability to grasp or be grasped by the poem in Spanish so resembled my inability to grasp or be grasped by the poem in English that I felt, in this respect, like a native speaker. So after I'd dismissed the Quixote, eaten, jacked off, read some Tolstoy, I carried what was left of the wine and an anthology of contemporary Spanish poetry onto the roof and read a few poems by what was left of the light.

As night fell La Plaza Santa Ana began to fill with tourists, and one could also see some Madrileños meeting up, kisses on both cheeks, although the locals weren't out in force until much later. You could hear several languages, American or Australian English to me the most grating, chairs scraping the pavement and cutlery scraping plates, glasses being collected from the metal tables or placed there, and usually a violinist, inoffensively unskilled. In the distance airliners made their way to Barajas, lights flashing slowly on the wing, the contrails vaguely pink until it was completely dark. I imagined the passengers could see me, imagined I was a passenger that could see me looking up at myself looking down.

In the first phase of my research, I knew no one except Jorge and his friends and they never invited me to do anything on weeknights; I'm not sure how they would have invited me, since I saw Jorge only on Fridays at the language school. I didn't have a phone, and they didn't know exactly where I lived. Since I had failed to attend any of the social events the foundation arranged, there was no one whose company I could join if I wanted to do the things one was supposed to do while in Madrid: progressing from one bar to another while getting progressively fucked up, then arriving at a multistory discoteca and dancing, if that's even the word, to horrible techno, making out for hours, hours, then having chocolate con churros and stumbling home near dawn. This was apparently routine for a remarkable range of ages; certainly people of several generations were out very late; kids were still playing in the plaza at midnight; the late middle-aged drank into the early morning. I was unaccustomed to such hours or so much public space. While I thought of myself as superior to all the carousal I was in fact desperate for some form of participation both because I was terribly bored at night and because I was undeniably attracted to the air's vulgar libidinal charge. Of course I could not sit in the plaza alone, although I saw men do that, guidebooks beside their beers, and I could not approach one of the innumerable roving bands and just ask to join their company, but I came to realize that I could leave my apartment and enter the flow of the night unashamed so long as I walked purposefully, pretending I had somewhere to be.

I would roll one or two spliffs and put them in a pack of cigarettes, drink a glass of water, brush my teeth, walk down the stairs and out of the apartment into the plaza. I felt as I crossed the plaza that I was observing myself from the roof of my apartment; from there I could see that I was walking too fast and I'd stop, light a spliff or cigarette, then resume walking at a less frantic pace toward Puerta del Sol, the literal center of the city, which I could reach in a few minutes. From Sol I would pause and decide where to pretend I needed to be.

Most often I walked down Gran Vía, where the prostitutes were out, smoking in front of the shuttered storefronts, dull glow of orange and purple lipstick, and eventually made my way into Chueca, a largely gay neighborhood known, so the guidebooks said, for its vibrant nightlife, but where there tended to be fewer Americans. The streets in Chueca were so narrow and its plaza so full in those months that it was easy to mill around in such a manner that people on your right assumed you were with the people on your left and vice versa. This was also true in its various overflowing bars; I could order a drink and stand looking bored in the middle of the bar and people would suppose I pertained to one of the adjacent parties; indeed, people in one large group or another often began to speak to me, assuming I was one of their number whom they hadn't had the chance to meet. Over the general din I could hear next to nothing, but I smiled and nodded and sometimes slightly raised my glass, and henceforth turned a little more toward the group whose member had addressed me; slowly, I would be absorbed.

Which is how I met Arturo, a turning point in my project. I was at a very crowded bar in Chueca, a mixed bar with Moroccan decor and sequined pillows everywhere, drinking a cloying mojito when he arrived and began greeting the group I was orbiting. He embraced me warmly after he embraced the others and, since I was the closest to the bar, asked if I wanted a drink. While we waited to be served he asked me how I knew so and so, who I assumed had convened the gathering. I shrugged in a way that indicated everybody knew so and so. Then he asked where I was from and I lied: New York. He said either that he had recently been to New York or that he was going to New York soon. For what, I asked. He answered for a musical performance, or to perform music, or for some sort of performance art. What are you doing in Madrid, he said. Here I delivered a version of the answer I had memorized for my Spanish exam in Providence, a long answer composed by a fluent friend, regarding the significance of the Spanish Civil War, about which I knew nothing, for a generation of writers, few of whom I'd read; I intended to write, I explained, a long, research-driven poem exploring the war's literary legacy. It was an answer of considerable grammatical complexity, describing the significance of my project in the conditional, the past subjunctive, and the future tense. To my surprise and discomfort Arturo's interest was piqued and he peppered me with questions: have you met so and so, the scholar or poet; have you visited such and such museum or archive. It's difficult to hear in this bar, I said. He ordered two beers and when they arrived he paid and motioned for me to follow him outside.

Outside we lit cigarettes and before he could repeat his questions I hurriedly said: my Spanish is not good. I read very well, I lied, but I don't speak. He laughed and asked if I knew various people and when I said no, he would say, with excitement, that he had to introduce me. You're very nice, I kept saying, which struck him as very funny. Fashionable people kept greeting him as they passed. He told me he owned or worked at a gallery in Salamanca, the ritziest neighborhood in the city, and that his brother or boyfriend was either a famous photographer, sold famous photographs, or was a famous cameraman. He said something about how his gallery was a place where poets gathered, held readings, and he spoke at length in terms I could barely follow about his own love for poetry, listing several Spanish poets of whom I'd never heard, plus the obligatory mention of Lorca. He gave me the gallery's card, first writing a cell phone number on one side of it, then put his arm around me warmly and returned me to the group inside the bar. There everyone assumed I was a friend of Arturo's and we exchanged names and, with the two women nearest me, Teresa and Ester, kisses on both cheeks. Arturo immediately entered into conversation and I slipped away to the bar to order another mojito, and every time thereafter I thought I might be called upon to speak, I absconded to the bar. I would ask, largely by indicating my glass or theirs and raising my eyebrows, if I could bring anyone anything; Ester disappeared after a while but I bought Teresa and Arturo several mojitos and it was when I found myself enthusiastically explaining my project to Teresa that I realized I had had too many.

I need air, I said, and left the slowly spinning bar; I intended to walk home and pass out. While I was leaning against the wall of the bar collecting myself for the walk I was surprised to find Arturo and Teresa suddenly beside me, asking if I was all right. Yes, I said, and straightened myself abruptly, causing the spins to resume, redouble; I realized I would vomit. I walked across the street where there were fewer people and a public trash can and, just before I reached it, vomited indeed. When I finished being sick, I stood up and there they were just across the street, waiting for me, Teresa smoking and Arturo proffering a bottle of water, smiling. I crossed, washed out my mouth, drank some of the water, and thanked him. We'll drive you home, he said, we're going to another party anyway.

I was embarrassed to tell Arturo once we were in his car that I was a ten-minute walk from home, but, as it turned out, I didn't have to tell him anything; the joint Teresa lit and passed back to me produced a cone of intense heat in my throat, which then migrated to my chest, where it unfurled against my rib cage. I realized my tongue was numb or at least tingling and I couldn't summon the name of my street, a situation that struck me as horrifying and hilarious. I turned my head and watched the lights slide by and found it lovely and then I realized I was saying so in English, that several minutes had elapsed and I was enumerating everything I found beautiful as we passed; streetlights, fountains, plane trees, if that's what those were. While in the first phase of my project I very rarely spoke Spanish, I had almost never had occasion to use my English, and the latter erupted as we left the city and merged onto a highway, Arturo and Teresa having decided to take me with them to the party; maybe I had asked. With what I thought was remarkable eloquence and rhythm I described Cyrus feeding bats at dusk in Providence and seeing myself from above; I elaborated something like a theory of poetry, deadest of all media, in cadences that rose and fell so movingly I imagined Arturo and Teresa would find themselves compelled to acknowledge my profundity, all the more compelled for not comprehending me, save for occasional cognates; they would experience the periodicity of my thinking without the distraction of particular thoughts. I was speaking grammar, pure and universal, but also suggesting a higher form of music: as I listened to myself I was amazed by the exquisite sonic patterning of my English, small changes rung on fricative and glide, and these subtle aural variations were little enactments of whatever the words denoted, language becoming the experience it described. At some point I passed out.

We were parked along with many other cars in a long circular drive-way and Arturo and Teresa were discussing something, Teresa playing with Arturo's hair, calling him Arturito. We sat in front of an aggressively modern house, low to the ground, expansive, white stone and acres of glass. I caught Teresa's eyes in the rearview mirror and she asked how I was. Arturo opened his door and we all got out of the car; I asked where we were and Arturo said, my boyfriend's. Teresa entered the house on my arm, whether out of irony because I was a drunken American idiot brought to the party as a joke, or because she felt a vague solicitude toward me after my strange performance in the car, I didn't know, but I could hope. As we entered the party I reminded myself to breathe. There were a lot of handsome people in the sweeping white-carpeted living room with minimalist furniture and monumental paintings on the carefully lit walls. Various people greeted us and Teresa detached from me to kiss them and I was acutely aware of not being attractive enough for my surroundings; luckily I had a strategy for such situations, one I had developed over many visits to New York with the dim kids of the stars: I opened my eyes a little more widely than normal, opened them to a very specific point, raising my eyebrows and also allowing my mouth to curl up into the implication of a smile. I held this look steady once it had obtained, a look that communicated incredulity cut with familiarity, a boredom arrested only by a vaguely anthro-pological interest in my surroundings, a look that contained a dose of contempt I hoped could be read as political, as insinuating that, after a frivolous night, I would be returning to the front lines of some struggle that would render whatever I experienced in such company null. The goal of this look was to make my insufficiencies appear chosen, to give my unstylish hair and clothes the force of protest; I was a figure for the outside to this life, I had known it and rejected it and now was back as an ambassador from a reality more immediate and just.

Teresa took my arm again and led me to a bar in one corner of the giant room; when we'd fixed drinks, she walked me out onto a vast patio where there was another bar and a large teardrop-shaped pool, faintly illuminated, its floor blue tile, in which more handsome people, a few women topless, splashed around. As I tried to hold the look, Teresa led me beyond the pool into a rock garden of some sort where there was a smaller group of people organized around a central figure singing and playing the guitar, the performer on a stone bench, the others on the ground, Arturo already among them; we sat down.

There ensued a battle between the music and my face. I was at first put off and threatened by the handsome countenances of the other listeners, faces that displayed an absorption I refused to believe was felt, each face carefully positioned to imply a lively interior world, faces that invited others to admire their obliviousness to others. The men tended to look down, the women slightly up; the former as if in painful concentration, the latter beatific, half-smiling, but close to tears—everyone seemed to be having a profound experience of art. Several joints were being passed among these various private worlds and I was returning to my previous heights, losing coordination in my face, my eyes still wide but now a little too wide, the hint of smile lost and with it all suggestion of detachment.

As I struggled to recompose my aspect I began to hear the music, to hear it as addressing me and not just as an excuse for the other faces to assume their poses. He was an unmistakably good singer, his range and control bespeaking years of training, not that I would know, and his guitar competent and understated in a way that showed he was an experienced performer, not competing with himself. He was careful not to raise his voice, or to let it raise itself a little on its own, and he had a delicate lilt, his phrasing wavering between speech and song, mundanity and sorrow, the melody reasserting itself only to dissolve. The lyrics were composed almost entirely of vowels and it took me a while to realize the song was Portuguese, not Spanish; I experienced the slow shading of one language into another, a powerful effect only my ignorance of both enabled. As I listened the day rewound, but not just my day: the drive, the bar, the roof of my apartment, seeing myself on the roof from a plane, boarding that plane in New York, leaving Providence, arriving in Providence when I was eighteen, etc., all the way back to Bright Circle Montessori, my dad gentle but insistent that I had to leave the car. Then Teresa was playing with my hair, as she'd been playing with Arturo's, and I looked at her and felt an agitation I could not name. I stood quickly but quietly and left the group, walking farther away from the house and party and into the dark until I reached a wooden fence, the end of the property and the beginning of a downward slope, a few lights far below.

I no longer felt much of anything as I smoked and looked back toward the group and saw that someone, probably Teresa, was approaching, the ember of her cigarette describing little circles as she walked, the ice audible in her glass as she drew nearer, and I realized with some anxiety that she would expect me to be upset, very moved, that I needed to be so in order to justify my abrupt departure from the others. I turned back toward the fence, licked the tips of my fingers, and rubbed the spit under my eyes to make it look like I'd been crying, repeating this until I felt there would be enough moisture to catch a little light or at least make my face damp to the touch. It was Teresa, humming the song as she approached. When she reached me she asked gently if I were o.k., what was bothering me. Fine, nothing, I said, but in a way I hoped confirmed incommunicable depths had opened up inside me. We stood side by side looking down the slope and because I felt she was waiting for me to say something, I said: This is a difficult time for me. It was a stupid thing to say, but it was the only sentence I could form sufficiently freighted with mystery. Why, she asked, which surprised me, and I tried to calibrate my silence to convey less that I wasn't comfortable telling her than that the circumstance wasn't tellable, save maybe by guitar, certainly exceeding my Spanish, if not language in general. Tell me, she said and started to do the thing with my hair again and I thought she could see the wetness on my cheeks and I said, I was shocked to hear myself say: My mother died.

Poor boy, poor boy, Teresa said, embracing me, and I let my head rest on her shoulder, careful to touch her skin where my face was wet; her skin was warm, almost hot. At first I felt something like accomplishment at my performance and excitement at the contact with her body but this quickly gave way to a sinking feeling as I began to imagine my mom, how she would feel if she knew what I had done, my self-disgust giving way in turn to the fear that some-how this lie would have material effects, would kill her, or at least that, when something did in fact happen to my mother, as happen it must, I would always feel and be at least in part responsible, that whatever she suffered would be traceable in some important sense to this exact moment when I traded her life for the sympathy of an attractive stranger. I began to cry, both arms around Teresa now, real tears falling down her back as she hummed to comfort me, maybe believing me only then. When my tears subsided, we both sat down and looked out over the slope in silence. She lit a cigarette and passed it to me and began to speak.

She described the death of her father when she was a little girl, or how the death of her father turns her back into a little girl whenever she thinks of it; he had been young when he died but seemed old to her now, or he had been old when he died but in her memories grew younger. She began to quote the clichés people had offered her about what time would do, how he was in a better place, or maybe she was just offering these clichés to me without irony; then she began to talk about how Arturo had taken it, so I guessed he was her brother, about describing heaven to Arturo, how daddy was in heaven, so I guessed that he was younger. The father had been either a famous painter or collector of paintings and she had either become a painter to impress him or quit painting because she couldn't deal with the pressure of his example or because he was such an asshole, although here I was basically guessing; all I knew was painting was mentioned with some bitterness or regret. Then without a transition or with a transition I missed she was talking about her travels in Europe and then I heard her say New York and college and she paused and as she paused my breath caught because I realized what was coming.

In fluent English she described how one night she went alone to a movie somewhere in the Village, a boring movie, she couldn't even remember which, but when she left the movie and was debating whether to take a train or a cab back uptown the full reality of her father's death, it had been around a year, was suddenly and for the first time upon her, and she began to cry and found a pay phone and called her mother and cried and cried and eventually her calling card ran out and she went and bought another from a kiosk and returned to the phone and called her mother and cried into the phone until the second calling card ran out. She said she often wondered if that pay phone was still there, now that everyone uses cell phones, and then faced me smiling and said that when I was back home in New York I could look for it and if it was still there I could buy a calling card and call her and we could cry together for my mom.

2

I THOUGHT I HAD MADE IT CLEAR TO ARTURO OVER THE COURSE OF several conversations that I would not read, that I would be happy to come to the reading, but only to listen, not that I'd understand much of what I was hearing, and while I was very flattered that he wanted to attempt translations of my poetry, I was too shy and ambivalent about my "work" in its current state to read with his accompaniment at the gallery. I was embarrassed I'd given in to his repeated requests to see my writing in the first place, writing that I'd photocopied for him out of my notebook, and which I assumed he read with Teresa's help, as his English was terrible, just a smattering of phrases. But when he picked me up and saw me empty-handed, he told me to hurry and get my poems, that we were already late, and he was so insistent that I found myself running back up the stairs, thinking maybe he just needed to make another copy, and I grabbed my notebook and bag, and then reiterated as we drove toward the gallery that I wasn't going to read; claro, he kept saying, which means sure.

It was getting cold; I had somehow never thought Madrid would have a winter, but I was sweating, no doubt visibly, as Arturo greeted and introduced me to the shivering smokers milling around the gallery's glass doors. I was too nervous to catch the names of the people with whom I exchanged handshakes, but I was aware that my kissing was particularly awkward, that I had kissed one of the women on the corner of her mouth, more on her lips than on her cheek. This was a common occurrence; with a handful of clumsy exceptions when I had met particularly cosmopolitan New Yorkers one kiss on the right cheek, and various relatives when I was a child, I had almost never, prior to my project, kissed a woman with whom I was not romantically involved. I wasn't exactly sure what would have happened if I'd tried to greet a woman by kissing her in Topeka; certainly her boyfriend would kick in my teeth if she had one, or I would be at risk of becoming her boyfriend if she didn't. It often occurred to me that my upbringing would have been changed beyond all recognition if kissing had been common; such a dispersion of the erotic into general social circulation would have had unpredictable effects. In Providence I could have gotten away with it, but not without an air of affectation and effeminacy; regardless, I had never thought to try. But in Spain I was guilty of abusing the kissing thing, or of at least investing it with a libidinal charge it wasn't supposed to contain, and when you were drunk or high and foreign, you could reasonably slip up and catch the corner of the mouth.

We entered the gallery and I saw Teresa and Rafa, Arturo's boyfriend, standing next to a table with tapas and wine. I was heading in their direction, considering breaking my rule and speaking English to Teresa, asking her to explain to Arturo that I would not read and why, when I recognized, to my horror and surprise, María José from the foundation among the people perusing the gallery walls, which featured glossy black-and-white photographs of idle industrial machinery. I had met her only twice, once upon my arrival to fill out paperwork and once to turn in a brief report in English about my activities so far, a report upon which my stipend's continued disbursement depended; both encounters were sufficiently uncomfortable to have rendered her image indelible. I had been convinced that she could see through me, that my fraudulence was completely apparent to her, which wouldn't have required too much perspicacity on her part given the state of my Spanish, and given the fact that each time she recommended, as a way of making small talk, a poet or authority on the Spanish Civil War, I blinked and said something about the name sounding familiar, although I wasn't sure I used the right word for "familiar."

She saw that I saw her and approached me smiling and we exchanged kisses far from the mouth and she said something about the opportunity to hear my work, an opportunity I thought she said was particularly welcome because she hadn't seen me at any of the foundation's social events. Then she indicated some other Americans who I assumed were also foundation fellows; they were speaking very competent Spanish, much better than mine, but speaking it too loudly, and I managed to ask how she had heard about the reading. Apparently the gallery had added the foundation to its e-mail list starting with "my" reading.

I managed to disengage from María José and kissed Teresa and embraced Rafa and stared as coldly as possible at Arturo while I tried to figure out an escape. Arturo patted my shoulder and said everything would be fine and started flipping through his own notebook, which I assumed contained the translations, and asked me which poems I planned to read. I thought about claiming I was too ill to continue, surely I looked sufficiently pale, but I was worried that failing to appear in front of María José would somehow constitute the breaking point of my relationship with the foundation, that the total vacuity of my project would finally be revealed and I would be sent home in shame. My mouth was dry and I poured myself a glass of white wine and said I didn't care which poems I read but that I would only read one or two. Teresa said to read the one about seeing myself on the ground from the plane and in the plane from the ground and I said, in my first expression of frustration in Spanish, that the poem wasn't *about* that, that poems aren't *about* anything, and the three of them stared at me, stunned. I said I was sorry, drained and refilled my glass, noting that Teresa seemed genuinely hurt; I found that to be a greater indication of her affection for me than the fact that she had favorites among my poems. We'll read it, I said.

Everyone began to take their seats; the gallery was long and narrow with high ceilings and white walls and it was full; there were probably eighty people. There was a podium with a lamp and microphone and a small pitcher of water and as I sat with Teresa and Rafa in the fourth row, pissed off, nauseated with anxiety, searching my bag for a tranquilizer as inconspicuously as possible, Arturo approached the podium, thanked everyone for coming, then talked about the night's program. We were lucky to have two of the most interesting new voices in Spanish and American poetry in the gallery. We would first hear from Tomás Gomez or Gutiérrez, who had won such and such prizes, and whose work had such and such characteristics, and who was also a talented painter. Then we'd hear from Adam Gordon, who was in Madrid on a prestigious fellowship, whose work was having some sort of effect on something, whose poetry was intensely political and reminiscent of a Spanish poet I'd never heard of, only instead of protesting Franco, it took on the United States of Bush. This amplified my nervousness, as it had nothing to do with my poetry, such as it was, and as Arturo sat down to applause and Tomás Gomez or Gutiérrez approached the podium, I imagined beating Arturo's face in with the microphone or lamp.

Tomás looked less like he was going to read poetry and more like he was going to sing flamenco or weep; he did not say thank you or good evening or anything but instead paused dramatically as if to gather his strength for what would be by any measure a heroic undertaking. He had shoulder-length hair that kept falling in his eyes as he arranged his papers and he kept smoothing it back with a gesture I found studied; he struck me as a caricature of himself, a caricature of El Poeta. A few more people were trickling into the gallery and he looked at them gravely until they found seats. Then he looked back down at his paper, looked back up at the crowd, and when the silence had intensified to his liking, he uttered what I assumed was the title of his first poem: "Sea." To my surprise this poem was totally intelligible to me, an Esperanto of clichés: waves, heart, pain, moon, breasts, beach, emptiness, etc.; the delivery was so cloying the thought crossed my mind that his apparent earnestness might be parody. But then he read his second poem, "Distance": mountains, sky, heart, pain, stars, breasts, river, emptiness, etc. I looked at Arturo and his face implied he was having a profound experience of art.

Maybe, I wondered or tried to wonder, I'm not understanding; maybe these words have a specific weight and valence I cannot appreciate in Spanish, or maybe he is performing subtle variations on a sexist tradition of which I am not in possession. As Tomás read a third poem, "Work Dream" or "Dream Work," I forced myself to listen *as if* the poem were unpredictable and profound, as if that were given somehow, and any failure to be compelled would be exclusively my own. The intensity of my listening did at least return strangeness to each word, force me to confront it as a sound, and then to recapture the miracle of sound opening or almost opening onto sense, and I managed to suspend my disgust. I could not, however, keep this up; it required too much concentration to hear such familiar figurations as intensely strange, even in Spanish. It was not until I began to consider the scene more generally that my interest caught: there were eighty or so people gathered to listen to this utter shit as though it were their daily language passing through the crucible of the human spirit and emerging purified, redeemed; or here were eighty-some people believing the commercial and ideological machinery of their grammar was being deconstructed or at least laid bare, although that didn't really seem like Tomás's thing; he was more of a crucible of the human spirit guy. If people were in fact moved, convincing themselves they discovered whatever they projected into the hackneyed poem, or better yet, if people felt the pressure to perform absorption in the face of what they knew was an embarrassing placeholder for an art no longer practicable for whatever reasons, a dead medium whose former power could be felt only as a loss—these scenarios did for me involve a pathos the actual poems did not, a pathos that in fact increased in proportion to their failure, as the more abysmal the experience of the actual the greater the implied heights of the virtual. Then I was able to hear the perfect idiocy of Tomás's writing as a kind of accomplishment, especially combined with his unwitting parody of himself, doing that thing with his hair, gripping the podium as though the waves of emotion breaking over him might wash him from his feet, and I began to relax a little about my own performance, the tranquilizer no doubt also having its effect. I told myself that no matter what I did, no matter what any poet did, the poems would constitute screens on which readers could project their own desperate belief in the possibility of poetic experience, whatever that might be, or afford them the opportunity to mourn its impossibility. My own poetry, I told myself, would offer this to the gathering as, or even more effectively, than Tomás's, as my poems in their randomness and disorder were in some important sense unformed, less poems than a pile of materials out of which poems could be built; they were pure potentiality, awaiting articulation. And translation would further keep my poems in contact with the virtual, as everyone must wonder what Arturo or Spanish was incapable of carrying over from the English, and so their failure, their negative power, was assured.

Tomás's increasingly histrionic manner signaled his reading was drawing to a close, and after yet another terrible poem he paused, looked at the audience again, and then abandoned the podium without a word, at which point everyone applauded. When the applause died down Arturo nodded to me. We approached the podium and he explained that I would read the poem in English and then he would offer the translation. He might also have claimed that, even if one had no English, some of the power of the original would be palpable. While he was saying this or something like it I poured myself a glass of water, nearly spilling it when I drank, and opened my notebook. When he turned and looked at me to signal I should start, I said thank you into the microphone and began to read my poem, to read it in a deadpan and monotonic but surprisingly confident way, considering my knees were shaking and my hands were freezing, to read it as if either I was so convinced of the poem's power that it needed no assistance from dramatic vocalization, or, contrarily, like it wasn't poetry at all, just an announcement of some sort: this train is delayed due to trackwork ahead, etc. I fantasized as I listened to myself that the undecidability of my style—was it an acknowledgment of the poem's intrinsic energy or a reading appropriate to its utter banality—would have its own kind of power, especially in Tomás's wake:

> *Under the arc of the cello*
> *I open the Lorca at random*
> *I turn my head and watch*
> *The lights slide by, a clearing*
> *Among possible referents*
> *Among the people perusing*
> *The gallery walls, dull glow*
> *Of orange and purple, child*
> *Behind glass, adult retreating*
> *I bit hard to deepen the cut*
> *I imagined the passengers*
> *Could see me, imagined I was*
> *A passenger that could see me*
> *Looking up . . .*

When I finished my portion of the reading I returned to my seat as the crowd applauded and then I realized I was no doubt supposed to stand with Arturo as he read his translations, but I was too relaxed now to rejoin him at the podium.

Arturo hesitated and I imagined he had expected my performance to be more like Tomás's than it was, had undertaken the translation with a much more dramatic performance in mind, and now he was trying to figure out if he needed to read the translation in the manner in which I'd read the original or if he should deliver it as he had envisioned it prior to my reading; I was glad to see him struggle. Then he began to read the translation in what he must have thought was the midpoint between my style and Tomás's, gripping the podium like the latter, but modeling my detachment, which had the strange and appropriate effect of making his voice sound dubbed.

At first I heard only so many Spanish words, but nothing I could recognize as my own; after all, there was nothing particularly original about my original poems, comprised as they were of mistranslations intermixed with repurposed fragments from deleted e-mails. But as the poem went on I slowly began to recognize something like my voice, if that's the word, a recognition made all the more strange in that I'd never recognized my voice before. Something in the arrangement of the lines, not the words themselves or what they denoted, indicated a ghostly presence behind the Spanish, and that presence was my own, or maybe it was my absence; it was like walking into a room where I was sure I'd never been, but seeing in the furniture or roaches in the ashtray or the coffee cup on the window ledge beside the shower signs that I had only recently left. Not that I'd ever owned that particular couch or cup, but that the specific disposition of those objects, the way they had been lived with, required or implied me; not that I was suffering from amnesia or déjà vu, but that I was both in that room and outside of it, maybe in the park, and not just in the park, but also in innumerable other possible rooms and parks at once. Any contingent object, couch or cup, "orange" or "naranja," could form the constellation that I was, could form it without me, but that's not really right; it was like seeing myself looking down at myself looking up.

When Arturo finished reading there was a long pause followed by what I experienced as unusually loud applause, and Arturo gestured toward me, redirecting that applause, and then said something about Tomás into the microphone, the applause thickening to include him before it gradually tapered off. People rose from their seats and either left to smoke, I guess smoking was bad for the art, or broke for the wine and tapas. Teresa approached and congratulated me and said I had done a wonderful job. Rafa embraced me, Rafa never really talked, and then I saw that María José was waiting to speak with me, American fellows in tow.

I introduced Teresa to María José and vice versa, and Teresa let fly a barrage of compliments about my writing and said something about how wonderful it was that the foundation had brought me to Madrid. While I couldn't understand much of what she was saying, it was clear it was eloquent, that Teresa spoke not as a friend but as a self-appointed representative of Spanish Art, and that María José was impressed, if a little put off. To me María José said she had enjoyed the reading very much, she looked forward to talking with me about how my new poems related to my research about the Spanish Civil War, perhaps at one of the upcoming events where fellows would be presenting their work, and I blinked a few times and said claro. Then one of the fellows introduced herself and said she too was a poet, basically yelled it, and that she would love to have coffee sometime and talk Spanish poetry. I blinked at her as well, but, before I could say claro, Arturo was pulling me away from the group to introduce me to Tomás, who had the air of a man badly misunderstood.

We shook hands and I said I liked your reading and he thanked me but didn't say anything back, I guess because he didn't like my poetry and because Tomás couldn't lie for the sake of politeness when it came to the most sacrosanct of arts. I was surprised how furious I became and how fast, but I didn't say anything; I just smiled slightly in a way intended to communicate that my own compliment had been mere graciousness and that I in fact believed his writing constituted a new low for his or any language, his or any art.

When I felt my face had made its point, I left him without saying excuse me, walked out of the gallery, and stood a few feet apart from the other smokers and lit my own cigarette, impervious to the cold. I sensed that the other smokers were whispering about me in respectfully hushed tones, and while I knew this was less because of any particular response they'd had to my reading than because I had been presented to them as a significant foreign writer, it nevertheless felt good. Eventually one of the group approached me and introduced himself as Abel. We shook hands and he said he enjoyed the reading, then explained that his photographs were hanging in the gallery and I said, although I hadn't really seen them, that they were excellent. Perhaps because I paid him this compliment as if my knowledge of photography were considerable, he seemed eager to demonstrate some understanding of poetry, and he began to compare my writing with a Spanish writer I didn't know. As he grew increasingly animated another smoker joined us, and after listening for a while he began to disagree with Abel, lightly at first, then with increasing intensity. The more heated the exchange, the more rapid the speech, and the less I understood; in the afterglow of what increasingly felt like my triumphant reading, however, I had the confidence to conduct or project a translation of pure will, and I came to believe I could follow the back and forth, which had the arc and feel of debates I'd heard before.

The poet to whom Abel likened me was a reactionary, the second smoker seemed to say, and his formal conservatism was the issue of his right-wing sympathies; my writing recalled him only in its sonority, but my formal openness signaled a supple capacity to take the measure of contemporary experience quite distinct from so-and-so's fascistic longing for some lost social unity. My work, said the second smoker, was much more reminiscent of another poet, whose name I'd never heard, who fled Franco and died in exile, a poet whose capacity to dwell among contradictions without any violent will to resolution formally modeled utopian possibility. This Abel dismissed with a wave of his cigarette as a simplistic, knee-jerk association of formal experimentation with left-wing politics, when in fact the leading Modernist innovators were themselves fascists or fascist sympathizers, and in the context of U.S. imperialism, I thought he argued, reestablishing forms of sufficient complexity and permanence to function as alternatives to the slick, disposable surfaces of commodity culture was the pressing task of poetry.

One cannot overcome the commodification of language by fleeing into an imagined past, the second smoker might have countered, which is the signature cultural fantasy of fascism, but rather one must seek out new forms that can figure future possibilities of language, which was what my work was somehow doing, unbeknownst to me, placing recycled archival materials in provocative juxtaposition with contemporary speech. We were all in one group now, the smokers, many of whom were lighting second or third cigarettes, and it was clear that I was expected to weigh in. I said or tried to say that the tension between the two positions, their division, was perhaps itself the truth, a claim I could make no matter what the positions were, and I had the sense the smokers found this comment penetrating.

I lit another cigarette to help my aperçu sink in, and in the ensuing silence I tried hard to imagine my poems' relation to Franco's mass graves, how my poems could be said meaningfully to bear on the deliberate and systematic destruction of a people or a planet, the abolition of classes, or in any sense constitute a significant political intervention. I tried hard to imagine my poems or any poems as machines that could make things happen, changing the government or the economy or even their language, the body or its sensorium, but I could not imagine this, could not even imagine imagining it. And yet when I imagined the total victory of those other things over poetry, when I imagined, with a sinking feeling, a world without even the terrible excuses for poems that kept faith with the virtual possibilities of the medium, without the sort of absurd ritual I'd participated in that evening, then I intuited an inestimable loss, a loss not of artworks but of art, and therefore infinite, the total triumph of the actual, and I realized that, in such a world, I would swallow a bottle of white pills.

———

We tended to wake at the same time, Isabel and I, which gave us the sense of having been awoken by something, a noise external or internal to our dreams, and we listened, facing each other, blinking, for the noise to recur, which it didn't, although I never mentioned this idea about the noise to her, so she might not have had the experience I ascribed her. She would get out of bed and wrap herself in the towel that was always draped across the chair, then shower while I put on the coffee. When the coffee was ready I would say so loudly enough that she could hear me over the water and she would turn off the water and rewrap herself in the towel and we'd take our coffee on the couch and smoke, moving the little butane heater close to us. Then I showered and did the things I didn't do in front of her: shit, take pills, and when I came out of the bathroom she would be dressed, putting up her hair.

She was always wrapping or unwrapping her hair or body in some sort of cloth, winding or unwinding a shawl or scarf, and whenever I imagined her, I imagined her engaged in one of these activities; I couldn't picture her standing still, fully dressed or undressed, but only in the process of gracefully entangling or disentangling herself from fabric. I tried to tell her this, as I thought it would sound poetic, but I didn't have any of the relevant verbs, so I said something about not having the words to describe how she was always moving, how I couldn't imagine her still, and I made a series of gestures that communicated this was a pale version of what I had intended to communicate, and left her to unfold my meaning.

Except for our most basic exchanges, pass me this or pass me that, what time is it, and so on, our conversation largely consisted of my gesturing toward something I was powerless to express, then guessing at whatever referent she guessed at, and gesturing in response to that. In this, my project's second phase, Isabel assigned profound meaning, assigned a plurality of possible profound meanings, to my fragmentary speech, intuiting from those fragments depths of insight and latent eloquence, and because she projected what she thought she discovered, she experienced, I liked to think, an intense affinity for the workings of my mind.

As we walked through the Reina Sofía I would offer up unconjugated sentences or sentence fragments in response to paintings that she then expanded and concatenated into penetrating observations about line and color, art and institutions, old world and new, or at least I imagined those expansions; To photograph a painting—, I said with derisive mystery as we watched the tourists in front of *Guernica,* and then I observed her face as this phrase spread out into a meditation on art in the age of technological reproducibility. I would say, Blue is an idea about distance, or Literature ends in that particular blue, or Here are several subjunctive blues; I would say, To write with sculpture—, To think the vertical—, To refute a century of shadow—, etc., and watch her mouth the phrase to herself, investing it with all possible resonances, then reapplying it to canvas. Of course we engaged in our share of incidental talk, but our most intense and ostensibly intimate interactions were the effect of her imbuing my silences, the gaps out of which my Spanish was primarily composed, with tremendous intellectual and aesthetic force. And I believe she imbued my body thus, finding every touch enhanced by ambiguity of intention, as if it too required translation, and so each touch branched out, became a variety of touches. Her experience of my body, I thought, was more her experience of her experience of her body, of its symphonic receptivity, ridiculous phrase, and my experience of my body was her experience once removed, which meant my body was dissolved, and that's all I'd ever really wanted from my body, such as it was.

Isabel did not own a car but there were apparently several cars to which she had access; weekends during the winter of my project she would drive us out of Madrid in a small red car, a small yellow car, or a brown station wagon to whatever nearby town might have a church or restaurant or relative of interest. She seemed to have innumerable aunts and cousins and, after visiting relics or yet another El Greco or eating partridge, baby pig, or some other regional delicacy lately slain, we would meet up with her family, smoke, and drink. I had been in Spain long enough that when I met her relations I felt compelled to appear more shy and reticent than monolingual; luckily, this was an impression it was easy to give, for as long as I remembered to change my expression in keeping with the tone of whoever was declaiming, I could affect comprehension, and if I spoke very quietly when I had to speak, and if I smoked a little sullenly, no one attempted to enlist me in conversation. This worked with everybody except her Aunt Rufina.

It was sunny but very cold on the day we drove to Toledo and I sensed from Isabel's manner that her relationship with Rufina was complex, at least she kept thinking out loud about whether we should in fact visit Rufina after walking around the city, if we would have time or if she might be busy, whereas we normally just showed up at one of her relations' houses or apartments, no matter the hour, and were absorbed with a flurry of kisses into whatever they were doing, usually drinking and watching TV. On the highway to Toledo we passed several tour buses full of what looked like Americans, digital cameras already in hand, and as we drew past them I expressed infinite disdain, which I could do easily with my eyebrows, for every tourist whose gaze I met. My look accused them of supporting the war, of treating people and the relations between people like things, of being the lemmings of a murderous and spectacular empire, accused them as if I were a writer in flight from a repressive regime, rather than one of its most fraudulent grantees. Indeed, whenever I encountered an American I showered him or her with silent contempt, and not just the loud, interchangeable frat boys calling each other by their last names, calling each other fags, and the peroxided, inevitably miniskirted sorority girls spending their junior year abroad, dividing their time between internet cafés and discotecas, complaining about the food or water pressure in the households of their host families, having chosen Spain over Mexico, where Cyrus was, because it was safer, cleaner, whiter, if farther from their parents' gated communities. I had contempt not just for the middle-aged with their fanny packs and fishing hats and whining kids, or the barbate backpackers who acted as though failing to shower were falling off the grid; rather, I reserved my most intense antipathy for those Americans who attempted to blend in, who made Spanish friends and eschewed the company of their countrymen, who refused to speak English and who, when they spoke Spanish, exaggerated the peninsular lisp. At first I was unaware of the presence in Madrid of these subtler, quieter Americans, but as I became one, I began to perceive their numbers; I would be congratulating myself on lunching with Isabel at a tourist-free restaurant, congratulating myself on making contact with authentic Spain, which I only defined negatively as an American-free space, when I would catch the eyes of a man or woman at another table, early twenties to early thirties, surrounded by Spaniards, reticent compared to the rest of the company, smoking a little sullenly, and I knew, we would both know immediately, that we were of a piece. I came to understand that if you looked around carefully as you walked through the supposedly least touristy barrios, you could identify young Americans whose lives were structured by attempting to appear otherwise, probably living on savings or giving private English lessons to rich kids, temporary expatriates sporting haircuts and clothing that, in hard-to-specify ways, seemed native to Madrid, in part because they were imperfect or belated versions of American styles. Each member of this shadowy network resented the others, who were irritating reminders that nothing was more American, whatever that means, than fleeing the American, whatever that is, and that their soft version of self-imposed exile was just another of late empire's packaged tours.

Toledo itself was lousy with tourists despite the fact that it was winter. We dodged and mocked them as we ascended the narrow streets toward the giant Alcázar, a stone fortification built on the city's highest point, which Isabel assumed I would find of particular interest because of its famous role in the Civil War, or at least its role in Nationalist lore: a bunch of fascists held out against the Popular Front, which laid siege to it, until Franco arrived with the Army of Africa, an early and highly symbolic victory for the Nationalist cause. As we walked around the giant structure, which had to be largely rebuilt after the war, she recounted facts I barely followed about historical figures of whom I'd never heard. Then she began to ask me questions about my project, which had never interested her before.

"How did you choose Spain over, for example, Chile?"

"So much has been written about Allende," I said, although I had only the vaguest sense of who Allende was.

"What makes the poem an effective form for a historical investigation?" I inferred from the words of hers I understood. I was surprised to find myself inclined to defend a project I'd never clearly delineated, let alone ever planned to complete, as opposed to conceding its total vacuity.

"The language of poetry is the exact opposite of the language of mass media," I said, meaninglessly.

"But why are Americans studying Franco," she asked, gesturing toward a group of Americans being led around the Alcázar, "instead of studying Bush?" She said it as if every American tourist were planning a monograph on El Caudillo.

"The proper names of leaders are distractions from concrete economic modes." I was trying to sound deep, hoping concrete and mode were cognates. My limited stock of verbs encouraged general pronouncements.

"Why aren't you studying the American economic mode?" She was angry.

"You can't study a mode of production *directly*." And with my manner, I said, "I am delivering a fact so obvious it pains me."

"I'm sure the people of Iraq are looking forward to your poem about Franco and his economy." It was the first unkind thing she'd ever said to me.

I met this with silence, so as to allow her to imagine an array of responses I was in fact incapable of producing, and I held this silence as we left the Alcázar and descended back into town toward the cathedral, where there were some famous El Grecos, although if I never saw his torturously elongated figures or phantasmagorical, sickly coloring again, it would have been too soon. What disturbed me as we walked was not that Isabel was pissed off, and certainly not that she thought my project was absurd or that she found me to be a typically pretentious American, but that our exchange, despite my best efforts, and perhaps for the first time, had involved much more of the actual than the virtual. I'd said, as usual, nothing of substance, but the nothing I'd said just languished between us; I didn't feel her opening it up into a chorus of possibilities, and the silence we were now maintaining was the mere absence of sound, not the swelling of potential meanings. This was in part because my Spanish was getting better, despite myself, and I experienced, with the force of revelation, an obvious realization: our relationship largely depended upon my never becoming fluent, on my having an excuse to speak in enigmatic fragments or koans, and while I had no fear of mastering Spanish, I wondered, as we walked past the convents and gift shops, how long I could remain in Madrid without crossing whatever invisible threshold of proficiency would render me devoid of interest.

It was early dusk by the time we reached the cathedral, and in a Spanish cathedral it always felt like dusk, dull gold and gray stone and indeterminate distances, so I had the feeling less of going indoors than of entering a differently structured but nonetheless exterior space. I was alarmed to find myself wanting to produce an elegant formulation of this experience for Isabel, alarmed not only because I couldn't formulate anything elegantly in Spanish, but because this was the first time in her company that I had desired to get my point across instead of attempting to make its depth a felt effect of its incommunicability. Now I feared I'd neither be able to be eloquent positively nor negatively and, as we made the rounds of the capillas, I realized with a sinking feeling that the reduction of our interactions to the literal and the transformation of our pregnant silences into dead air, a flat spectrum over a defined band, would necessarily strip my body of whatever suggestive power it had previously enjoyed, and that, when we made love, she would no longer experience her own capacity for experience, but merely my body in all its unfortunate actuality.

*I tried hard to imagine my poems or any poems as machines
that could make things happen.*

I could feel the initial creep of panic, and as I reached around in my
bag for a yellow tranquilizer, I encountered one of my notebooks,
which I took out; I found a pen and quickly jotted down the idea
about the dusk and the cathedral, aware and encouraged that Isabel
was watching as I wrote. I arranged my face into a look of intense concentration, a look that implied I'd had a lightning flash of intellection,
that there was no time to waste on speech as I hurried to give my
insight a more enduring form. Isabel broke our silence, maybe half an
hour old, to ask what I was writing, and I said I'd had an idea for a
poem, possibly an essay. She waited for me to elaborate, which I didn't,
and I believed she looked with real curiosity at my notebook as I
returned it to my bag. This, I thought to myself, as we finished our cir-
cuit around the cathedral and emerged into the darkling street, would
allow me to retain my negative capability, although that wasn't the

phrase; I could displace the mystery of my speech onto my writing, the latter perhaps recharging the former. If our conversations were no longer shot through with possibility, if what I said no longer resonated on many potential levels simultaneously, what I wrote in a language she could not read would have to preserve my aura of profundity. And since the raw material for these notes that were the raw material for poems emerged out of our time together, she would in some important if unnamable sense have a hand in their genesis; there would be traces of her presence, she might imagine, in subject or formal process. Indeed, if the poems did not prove powerful, maybe she shared in the responsibility, as it would mean, if she had faith in my talent, that our time together failed to inspire me, and why wouldn't she have faith in my talent, given that I'd attended a prestigious university and received a prestigious fellowship. She would experience the present as suffused with the possibility of eventual transfiguration into a poem, and this future poem was a fund each moment could draw upon; my notebook, not my fragmentary Spanish, would become the sign of the virtual, enabling my project to advance. I was so calmed and encouraged by this new narrative, I forgot about the tranquilizer, and as we walked toward the ramparts near where Isabel had parked, I said to her:

"I read my poems and a friend read translations at a gallery in Salamanca the other night." This was intended to hurt her a little and it seemed to. Since I'd never planned to read, I'd never thought to invite her, and besides, I had a policy of keeping Isabel away from Arturo and Teresa, not because I didn't think they'd like each other, but because I wanted them to believe I had an expansive social life. But I knew she would be stung to think I'd given a public performance without her, stung and impressed I was receiving such attention, and that all of this would improve her image of my poetry, lend it mystery, while also making her jealous of my other friends.

"The poems you read—what were they about?" she asked, after a long silence that said, "Why didn't you invite me?"

I was also silent for a while, then stopped and turned to her and put my hands on her shoulders, which I never did, and looked her in the eyes, which sounds ridiculous, and said, tenderly, "Poems aren't *about* anything."

"Poems aren't about anything," she repeated, largely to herself, perhaps with a hint of incredulity or bemusement or scorn, and it wasn't clear to me whether its significance was spreading out. I kissed her in case that helped the resonance expand.

By the time we reached the car I felt the balance of our relationship had been restored; I believed Isabel felt it too, and in a rush of optimism, she decided we should, in fact, visit Rufina. It was dark now as we drove across the ramparts and after fifteen minutes or so of confusing, curving roads, we pulled off into a gravel driveway. During the drive Isabel started and abandoned various descriptions of her aunt, attempting to avoid disparaging her in any way, which suggested affinity and respect, while also trying to warn me, it was unclear regarding what. Finally she managed, haltingly, to say something about a fight over Isabel's ex-boyfriend, a fight arising, I thought she said, from Rufina's protectiveness of Isabel, her sense that Isabel had been treated poorly, but a bad fight nonetheless.

Rufina's house was small, white, boxy, two stories, but set on a large expanse of land, which I assumed, during the day, offered prospects of the distant hills, or were those mountains. Dogs appeared as we approached the house, recognizing Isabel, who greeted them in the dark by name. We rang the bell and I could hear the radio inside. The door opened and Rufina appeared; I was stunned by her youth, she looked thirty, shapely, and was made up as if about to go out for the evening—eye shadow and lipstick, clothes that seemed selected carefully—despite the fact that she was in the country, alone. I thought she might have missed a beat between seeing us and greeting Isabel warmly, but the greeting was, when it came, very warm; as she held Isabel's face and wiped off her lipstick with her thumbs, I thought one or both of them might cry; Rufina was pressing hard. She released Isabel, kissed me quickly on both cheeks, and told us to come in, shutting out the dogs. We followed her into the kitchen where, without asking us what we wanted, she took out three tall glasses, gin from the freezer, and a bottle of tonic from the fridge. She put ice in the glasses and poured the cocktails in the Spanish manner, filling each glass almost entirely with gin, barely cutting it with tonic, then led us with our drinks to an enclosed and heated porch where we sat down in low cane chairs and near-dark.

I squinted at Rufina, waiting for my eyes to adjust. She and Isabel were obligatorily catching up, the Spanish so fast and full of slang I didn't even try to comprehend it; after a minute or two, the rush of small talk tapered into silence. Rufina took a long match from a box somewhere within her reach and lit a cigarette and I thought she looked mean and attractive in its light, her appeal perhaps amplified by the fact that I'd spent the day imagining a visit to an elderly aunt. Isabel looked nervous, adjusting her hair; it was clear this was the first time they'd seen each other since the aforementioned fight. Rufina held the match toward me, shook it out. Why Isabel had brought me I found baffling, she certainly made no effort to introduce me into the conversation; I could only suspect my presence was a restraint, that Isabel wanted to work out whatever was between them, and hoped Rufina would rein in her behavior and talk in the company of a stranger, especially talk about a previous boyfriend. The silence was evidently oppressive to Isabel, who knew I wouldn't break it, and finally she rose and said she had to go to the bathroom, leaving me with Rufina. I was in fact very interested in Rufina, in how she made a living, where she was from, how long she had lived outside Toledo and why, not to mention how old she was, if she was married, if she was Isabel's blood relation, what had happened with the boyfriend, etc., but I wasn't about to speak. After another length of silence, Rufina stood up, saying something about my drink, which she took to the kitchen to refill.

Alone on the porch, I looked out into the dark; I imagined I could see the dogs moving somewhere in the yard, and far beyond the yard I could see a few ruby taillights disappearing on a curve. I began to imagine my apartment in Madrid, imagined it at that instant, dark, but filled with noise from La Plaza Santa Ana, imagined the espresso machine at rest, the cheap but inoffensive furniture the apartment came with, furniture that would remain when I left, the few old postcards I'd purchased from El Rastro and scotch-taped to the wall. Then my other rooms: Brighton Street, mattress on the floor, Hope Street, with its little drafting table, dorms, which were terrible, then Greenwood, Jewell Street, Huntoon and my crib, which I could not in fact remember, imagined them at that instant, now furnished and occupied by others. Then I could feel each room around me as I imagined it, and the dark beyond the porch would become the dark of Topeka or Providence. Then it was the dark of my seventh or fifteenth or twentieth year, each dark with a slightly different shape or shapeliness, the sky, when I was younger, more concave. And then it was Rufina's porch again, but imagined from a future room surrounded by a future dark, a room where I was writing, maybe this.

At some point I realized I had been lost in these reveries, if that's what they were, for longer than it took to make a drink or take a piss. I listened hard and could hear voices, voices I could tell were raised; Isabel and Rufina were arguing somewhere in the house, in a room whose door they'd shut. I became fascinated with this phenomenon of hearing loud voices at a distance, in trying to account for how I knew they were loud when I could barely hear them, something about their shape or shapeliness, or the way they filtered through the walls, and I reached for my notebook to write this down, although there wasn't really light to write by, when suddenly I stopped and blushed, at least my face was hot. Why would I take notes when Isabel wasn't around to see me take them? I'd never taken notes before; I carried around my bag because of my drugs, not because I intended to work on my "translations," and the idea of actually being one of those poets who was constantly subject to fits of inspiration repelled me; I was unashamed to pretend to be inspired in front of Isabel, but that I had just believed myself inspired shamed me.

I took my notebook from the bag, but only to use it as a surface; I rubbed a cigarette between my thumb and forefinger to loosen the tobacco and emptied it onto the notebook cover. Then I took the little egg-shaped mass of hash out of my pocket, so shaped because it had been transported, wrapped in plastic, up someone's ass, found my lighter, heated and flaked a quantity of hash into the tobacco, then blew carefully into the empty cigarette paper, inflating it a little, and shook the mixture back into the cigarette, twisting the end of the paper to keep it from spilling. Finally, I removed the cottony filter with my teeth. The voices were getting louder.

I lit the spliff and imagined what was happening inside, my first projections borrowed almost entirely from Spanish cinema: Rufina and Isabel were lovers, Rufina maybe a transvestite, and Isabel had brought me to get back at Rufina for the latter's recent infidelity, but had underestimated Rufina; soon Rufina would return to the porch with a knife wet with Isabel's blood, stab me, then stab herself. Or Rufina, unspeakably wronged by unspeakable men, all of whom resembled Franco in some sense, had sworn that no man would ever cross the threshold of her home again, and Isabel had violated this rule, hoping, for whatever reason, to reintroduce Rufina to the opposite sex; soon Rufina would return with a knife wet with Isabel's blood, etc. As the hash had its effect, I took pleasure in picturing the flash of the knife reflected in Rufina's eyes, having to wrestle her into submission or die. I was relieved and disappointed, then, when a light came on and Rufina and Isabel returned to the porch, Rufina now wearing a gray oversized Hard Rock Café Houston sweatshirt and holding our refreshed drinks, Isabel relaxed and smiling.

"You smoked without us, Adán," Rufina exclaimed. She must have asked Isabel my name.

"I can make more," I said. "I can roll another," I corrected.

"So you're a poet, Adán," she ignored me. I just smiled. She repeated my name as if it were a one-word joke at my expense.

"He just read at a gallery in Salamanca," Isabel said to spite me.

"Salamanca—elegant!" It was clear Rufina was going to ask me what kind of poetry I wrote. "What kind of poetry do you write?"

"What kinds of poetry are there?" I was pleased with this response and made a mental note to use it from then on.

"Bad and worse," Rufina said with mock derision. Isabel laughed a little. Maybe it relaxed them further to be allied against me, to taunt the new boyfriend after clearing the air of the old.

"I, too, dislike it," I said in English.

"You must come from money," Rufina said, ignoring me again. Then she said something idiomatic involving hands and clouds, which I assumed was a colorful way of saying the same thing. "Do you have to work at all?"

I wasn't sure how to respond to this. I had encountered this association of poetry and money before in Spain, compounded, in my case, by the assumption that all Americans, I mean Americans abroad, were rich; compared to Isabel and Rufina, my family probably was. I had no clear sense of Isabel's class position, let alone Rufina's; I knew Isabel had graduated from college, had long worked at the language school, and now had a nice enough apartment, but she also had two roommates. I paid for almost all of our meals and drinks, but thought very little of it, even though it was a significant portion of my total funds, because euros always seemed fake to me. I had no idea, for instance, if the house we were in was of significant value, if land near Toledo was worthless or in high demand, if Rufina's manner of dress or address indicated the working or middle or some other class, or if those were the relevant terms for Spain.

"I won't have to work for several months, it's true," I said in a way that implied I would then have to work in a coal mine. "Unless you think writing is work."

"What will you do when you go back to the United States?" Rufina asked. Perhaps the most important unspoken rule that Isabel and I had developed in our short relationship, our most important kind of silence, was never to refer to the time after my fellowship. I looked at Isabel. It had been a while since I'd thought what I would, in fact, do upon my return.

"I don't know that I will go back," I lied. Isabel remained quiet, but there was a change in the intensity of her silence. I lit a cigarette to distance myself from this statement.

"And your parents will send you money," Rufina laughed, and then said something that involved the word "Bohemian." "What," she said, "do they do?"

I knew that no matter what I said my parents did, Rufina was going to find it hilarious, so I decided to tell the truth, although I knew it would be particularly funny: "They're both psychologists." I heard Isabel shift uncomfortably.

As expected, this cracked Rufina up. I assumed the flourish of talk that followed was about the preposterous image of a Bohemian poet supported by his psychologist parents. Isabel said something about not being too hard on me, but I smiled to indicate I was fine with being teased. "Isabel's friends from the language school are always rich," Rufina explained to me. "Friends" clearly meant "boyfriends."

"What is your profession?" I asked, sounding intensely foreign.

"I lost my job," she said, flatly. I blinked. "Maybe I'll start writing poetry. Maybe," she said, leaning forward and placing her hands on my thighs, "you'll marry me and we can live off your family." I thought I saw Isabel wince when Rufina touched me.

"O.K.," I said.

"Do you think your parents would like me?" Rufina asked, sticking out her chest in a performance of her voluptuousness I didn't quite understand, but enjoyed taking in.

"I think my mom and dad would like you," I said.

"I can cook and clean," she said, sarcastically, crossing and uncrossing her legs.

"My mom is a well-known feminist," I said, a statement that sounded as stupid as it was. Rufina laughed, Isabel asked what time it was, implying we should leave, but was ignored. I could see her staring at Rufina, mutely telling her to shut up; I didn't understand the extremity of her concern. "You'd like my mom," I said to get further away from the feminist thing, "but she's not so rich." I smiled again, in part to calm Isabel. "Neither she nor my father ever give me money,"

I lied. Now Isabel was looking at me strangely. I had just finished saying maybe Rufina could meet my parents if and when they visited Spain, when I remembered I'd told Isabel that my mom was dead.

There were several ways I could have recovered from this mistake; I could have looked melancholy and later claimed that I simply refused to share such a loss with Rufina, or, if I'd kept my cool, I could have maintained to Isabel that she had misunderstood my terrible Spanish in the first place, that I'd never said or meant to say that my mom had passed away. But I could feel my face, which was burning, fully confess to Isabel that I had lied to her. I'd told Isabel the lie during one of our first nights together when, still guilty from having recently told it to Teresa, I had felt compelled to repeat it, maybe to deepen my guilt into a kind of penance; surely I'd been drunk. Instead of amplifying my guilt, however, repetition mitigated it. While she had responded tenderly, Isabel never asked me about my family, and I never returned to it; at first I'd been aware of needing to avoid talking about my mother, as I still was with Teresa, but with Isabel I avoided talking about almost everything, save for my cryptic aesthetic pronouncements.

Isabel said she had to piss again and left the porch. Rufina, confused about what had passed between us, didn't resume her sarcastic inquiries, and in the ensuing silence, I tried to imagine how Isabel was going to react. My lie would be unforgivable in any context, but I felt it would be particularly unforgivable in Spain; had I told the lie about my father, that might have been o.k.; I could always say he was a fascist, whatever that meant, and that I'd merely engaged in wishful thinking. Almost every movie I had seen since arriving in Spain, maybe every Spanish movie made since 1975, was about killing, literally or symbolically, some pathologically strict, repressed, and violent father, or was at least about imagining a Spain without such men, a

Spain defined by liberated women rediscovering their joie de vivre with the help of their colorful gay friends. But to have "killed" my mother, the "feminist," for whatever reason, revealed me to be at heart a right-wing, jackbooted misogynist, and further called into question the legitimacy of my research.

"I told Isabel earlier," I said slowly to Rufina, who, smoking again, appeared to have forgotten all about me, "that my mother was dead. This isn't true."

"What?" she asked, suddenly interested, but sure she'd misunderstood.

"I told her my mom was dead, but my mom is alive," I paused. "Just now, I forgot I had lied."

"My God," Rufina said, and gasped. "Why did you do that, Adán?" She was more intrigued than disgusted. She was smiling, not unkindly.

"Because my mom is sick," I said. "And because—" I pretended it was difficult to go on. The smile drained quickly from her face. Then it was difficult to go on: "I am scared . . . I was trying to imagine . . ." Rufina leaned forward, now all tenderness. "I thought if I said it, I would have less fear," is how I must have sounded.

"Poor boy," Rufina said, and looked like she wanted to embrace me. The thrill I felt at her gaze checked the advancing waves of guilt. Isabel appeared in the door.

"I want to go," she said.

"Sit down, my love," Rufina said with an authority that returned Isabel to her chair. Then to me: "Continue."

"I came here," I began, "and nobody knows me. So I thought: You can be whatever you want to people. You can say you are rich or poor. You can say you are from anywhere, that you do anything. At first I felt very free, as if my life at home wasn't real anymore." Isabel was trying to make herself believe I'd confessed my lie to Rufina. "And I was glad to be away from my father," I threw in for color, implying my dad, gentlest of men, was some kind of tyrant. "But then the reality returns. And I have constant terror. I call her all the time. She says she is fine, but I don't know for sure. I didn't want to leave her, but she said I had to come here and do my work. That I had a responsibility to my writing. She insisted. I can't imagine life if something happens to her. And then when I meet someone important," I said, looking directly at Isabel, "I lied. To see. If I could say even the words." Isabel appeared to understand. "I am crazy, I know," I said, placing my head in my hands. Then I said, looking up at Isabel again, "I am sorry. I am sorry to her. I am sorry to you." I contemplated crying.

Isabel came to me and pulled my head against her and said something to comfort me that included the word "poet." Rufina was rubbing my leg. I saw myself as if from the yard, amazed.

———

That winter my research fell, my research was falling, into two equally unrepresentable categories. All December, there was rain, record amounts apparently; the city was strangely empty, emptied; even if it were merely drizzling, the Spaniards seemed to suspend all nonessential activity. Besides young men delivering the orange canisters of butane, or elderly women protected by plastic slickers hurrying between grocers, I saw next to no one on the streets. That December, if someone rang my buzzer, and that someone could only be Isabel, Teresa, or Arturo, their cars illegally parked in La Plaza Santa Ana, I wouldn't answer, and because it was raining, they wouldn't linger.

These periods of rain or periods between rains in which I was smoking and reading Tolstoy would be, I knew, impossible to narrate, and that impossibility entered the experience: the particular texture of my loneliness derived in part from my sense that I could only share it, could only describe it, as pure transition, a slow dissolve between scenes, as boredom, my project's uneventful third phase, possessed of no intrinsic content. But this account ascribed the period a sense of directionality, however slight or slow, made it a vector between events, when in fact the period was dilated, detached, strangely self-sufficient, but that's not really right.

During this period all like periods of my life were called forth to form a continuum, or at least a constellation, and so, far from forming the bland connective tissue between more eventful times, those times themselves became mere ligaments. Not the little lyric miracles and luminous branching injuries, but the other thing, whatever it was, was life, and was falsified by any way of talking or writing or thinking that emphasized sharply localized occurrences in time. But this was true only for the duration of one of these seemingly durationless periods; figure and ground could be reversed, and when one was in the midst of some new intensity, kiss or concussion, one was suddenly composed exclusively of such moments, burning always with this hard, gemlike flame. But such moments were equally impossible to represent precisely because they were ready-made literature, because the ease with which they could be represented entered and cancelled the experience: where life was supposed to be its most immediate, when the present managed to differentiate itself with violence, life was at its most generic, following the rules of Aristotle, and one did not make contact with the real, but performed such contact for an imagined audience.

This is what I felt, if it wasn't what I thought, as I smoked and listened to the rain on the roof and turned the pages and smelled the wet stone smell of Madrid through the windows I kept cracked. And when I read the *New York Times* online, where it was always the deadliest day since the invasion began, I wondered if the incommensurability of language and experience was new, if my experience of my experience issued from a damaged life of pornography and privilege, if there were happy ages when the starry sky was the map of all possible paths, or if this division of experience into what could not be named and what could not be lived just *was* experience, for all people for all time. Either way, I promised myself, I would never write a novel.

When it was raining in the afternoon I would sometimes walk through El Retiro, which would be empty save for a few hash dealers, all African, passing the time under the awning of a shuttered kiosk or, if it was only drizzling, standing under one of the steaming trees. There were always hash dealers in El Retiro, most of them around my age, selling eggs of what they called "chocolate," mainly to tourists, as there was much better hash to be had. I was surprised by how polite the polyglot dealers were, the prices highly negotiable in whatever language, no threat, however vague, of violence, and their sheer numbers startled me: one for every fifty yards of the park in good weather. While they must have known each other, one sensed that each man worked alone. As far as I could tell, the police tolerated the dealers in the park, although I'm sure they could be, and occasionally were, rounded up and deported. The police tolerated hash in general; I could never quite tell if it was legal or illegal to smoke. A policeman or park official of some sort might pass by on a golf cart, see you conversing with one of the dealers, and shoot you a dirty look, but never, in my experience, would he stop; if the look were dirty enough, the dealer might walk away from you, but typically with more annoyance than concern.

In the rainy period of my research, I would buy an egg or half an egg from whatever dealer I first encountered, the dealer surprised to have a customer in such weather, then walk to the semicircular colonnade built around the statue of Alfonso XII overlooking El Estanque. When I found a relatively dry, sheltered place, I smoked and watched the faint rain fall into the artificial lake. I had never smoked hash before coming to Spain and, unlike the weed I smoked in Providence, which instantly made me an idiot, the hash usually allowed me to maintain, or at least to believe I was maintaining, the semblance of lucidity, especially after months of habituation. I experienced it as a tuning of the world, not, as with strong weed, its total transformation or obliteration, and I could read or "work" while smoking hash, or at least believed I could, whereas when smoking stronger stuff I could not follow, let alone form, whole sentences. But the alterations effected by the hash were somehow all the more profound for being understated, in part because one could forget or at least discount the role of the drug in one's experience. If, say, a group of trees that had previously been mere background suddenly stood forth a little and their slender and strictly symmetrical forms became an elegant if unparaphrasable claim about form in general, you could write that observation down without dissolving it in the process, or without the strangeness of your hands distracting you from however you'd planned to use them. If a slight acoustic heightening allowed you to perceive for the first time consciously that the sound of the leaves in the wind was, as it were, in conversation with the similar but ultimately distinct sound of distant traffic on Calle de Alfonso XII, or that a hammering noise was in fact two noises, one issuing from a nearby tree and the other from a construction site beyond the park, and if these realizations inspired some meditation on the passing into one another of the natural and the cultural, the meditation, if not profound, could at least achieve coherence, could be formulated as it was experienced, not retrospectively, after coming down. Many people, I believed, used similar drugs to remove themselves from their experience, but because, for as long as I could remember, I always already felt removed from my experience, I took the drug to intensify the vantage from said remove, and so experienced it as an intensification of presence, but only at my customary distance from myself; maybe, when I panicked, that distance was collapsing.

That I smoked hash with tobacco was critical during this phase of my project, although I was resolved never to smoke a cigarette again after leaving Spain, and so smoked with particular abandon, critical because the cigarette or spliff was an indispensable technology, a substitute for speech in social situations, a way to occupy the mouth and hands when alone, a deep breathing technique that rendered exhalation material, a way to measure and/or pass the time. More important than the easily satisfiable addiction, what the little cylinders provided me was a prefabricated motivation and transition, a way to approach or depart from a group of people or a topic, enter or exit a room, conjoin or punctuate a sentence. The hardest part of quitting would be the loss of narrative function; it would be like removing telephones or newspapers from the movies of Hollywood's Golden Age; there would be no possible link between scenes, no way to circulate information or close distance, and when I imagined quitting smoking, I imagined "settling down," not because I associated quitting with a more mature self-care, but because I couldn't imagine moving through an array of social spaces without the cigarette as bridge or exit strategy. Happy were the ages when the starry sky was the map of all possible paths, ages of such perfect social integration that no drug was required to link the hero to the whole.

I didn't think these things, but might have, as I walked back through the park and home, then lay on my bed, only several feet beneath the downward-sloping ceiling, after having ignited the butane heater and drawn it near me. Once I was warm I would eat something, open a bottle of wine, and then write Cyrus, to whom I'd long since confessed I had internet access in my apartment, and who was in Mexico with his girlfriend and her dog. I was vaguely jealous of them; they'd driven to Mexico in her pickup with little money and no real plan in order to acquire experience, not just the experience of experience sponsored by my fellowship. His girlfriend, Jane, who had attended the same university as I, was the daughter of a very rich and famous man, but had foresworn her fortune, at least temporarily, in order to live lightly on the planet, make art, and write; before she left for Mexico, she had been squatting in one of Providence's abandoned warehouses with a group of like-minded artists. Often around eight or nine p.m. in Madrid, Cyrus would be in an internet café in Mexico, and we could instant message. One Monday night:

ME: you there? what's up in xalapa

CYRUS: Yeah. Went on a kind of trip this weekend. Planned to camp

ME: i was going camping here for a while

ME: hello?

CYRUS: I remember. It's hard to imagine you camping, I must say. Anyway, we drove to the country to see some pueblos, walk around

ME: cool

ME: what did you see

CYRUS: There was a bad scene there

ME: you mean a fight with jane?

CYRUS: No. Although we're fighting now, I guess

ME: stressful to travel together if you haven't before

CYRUS: Well we were walking

ME: still there?

CYRUS: along a river and

CYRUS: I'm still here, yes. Jane wanted to swim, but I was a little worried about the current. Not to mention the water did not strike me as particularly clean

ME: my brother once picked up a parasite swimming in a lake and was sick for a month

CYRUS: Right. And Jane launched into this speech about—half joking—about how I was afraid of new experiences or something, how I was always happier as a spectator. Not a fight, just teasing, albeit

ME: i hate new experiences

CYRUS: emasculating teasing. Something about that being what was wrong with poets

ME: the new poems are great, btw

CYRUS: I guess I should mention we were smoking a lot of that Acapulco Gold

ME: so what happened with

CYRUS: or whatever it is. Very staticky. Or at least I'd been smoking it. Vaguely reminiscent, incidentally, of certain Topeka strains, but more powerful. Anyway we walked along the river and it eventually opened out and where it was wider we encountered some people swimming

ME: americans?

CYRUS: Locals. There are no tourists here in winter, it seems

ME: right

CYRUS: There were two men swimming, or one swimming and one more like wading. The current looked pretty strong. One of the men, his girlfriend was on the bank—in a swimsuit—and he was trying to convince her to get in, to swim

ME: don't like where this is going. she was scared of the current?

CYRUS: Maybe. Maybe just the cold

ME: what is the weather like there

ME: madrid: cold and raining constantly

CYRUS: Warm to hot. It was like 80. Which is unseasonably warm, I guess. The air is filthy. But the water still chilly. Anyway, Jane—we were on the opposite bank as the swimmer's girlfriend—Jane wanted to swim

ME: she had a swimsuit?

CYRUS: and did get in the water, although I told her I didn't think

CYRUS: Yes, we both had swimsuits on under our clothes. It was not, I told her, a good idea, because of the current

ME: knowing her, i'm sure that was a goad

ME: might egg her on

CYRUS: Yes. She got in and while the current was strong was fine. Then the other swimmers, they were saying to the girlfriend, see, this girl got in, no problem, and then Jane started telling me to come into the water. So there I was opposite the girlfriend on the bank, both of us being pressured by the swimmers to join them. The girlfriend and I kept looking at each other with nervous smiles

ME: if one of you got in the other would have to

CYRUS: I felt that

ME: a game of chicken. you two should have left the others and gone off and had

CYRUS: Or at least if she got in I would have to. But she probably could have remained on the bank

ME: a wonderful life together!

ME: right. she would not be emasculated

CYRUS: but I was, I admit, feeling the pressure. Jane was there with these other men in the water, the current clearly manageable. I felt cowardly and American

ME: you have to stay strong—cowardice of your convictions

CYRUS: Yeah, well, I got in. The current was actually stronger than I imagined. There were pockets of strong current. Where the river narrowed a little farther down I could see what looked like serious rapids

ME: and then the girlfriend jumped in

CYRUS: Well

CYRUS: not at first. But now everyone kind of turned to her. We'd all become one group, somehow. And her boyfriend had changed from teasing her to encouraging her, his arms open, lovingly—it's fine, I promise, I'll protect you, etc. We were

ME: how bad is this going to get?

CYRUS: also encouraging her, I think. And laughing and screaming at the cold she jumped in. She was fine at first

ME: !

CYRUS: but as she kind of splashed around—she didn't really know how to swim, it didn't seem. I don't know, she moved somewhat downriver where the current became pretty strong, and she was getting upset

ME: so someone went and helped her?

CYRUS: Things

CYRUS: things got very bad very fast. she went under-water for a second, and when she resurfaced, she was a little farther down and totally panicked

ME: jesus

CYRUS: She was screaming and water was

ME: jesus

CYRUS: getting in her mouth and she was struggling against the current in the wrong way

ME: couldn't somebody get her

CYRUS: Her boyfriend was trying but there were enough stones and other shit that it was taking awhile. And he wasn't much of a swimmer either, didn't know, I don't think, what to expect from or how to manage the rapids. Jane tried to go

ME: tried to catch her?

CYRUS: Yes. I held her back. As I was holding her back I saw the girlfriend go under again, then reemerge briefly another, I don't know, ten feet down

ME: fuck

CYRUS: where the rapids were intense, and then she was really swept downriver. So

CYRUS: so Jane and I ran back onto the bank and to the truck and then, yelling something about what we were doing to the other swimmers—the friend was holding the boyfriend back who was now screaming—screaming in a very primal way, you understand—not screaming words. So we drove downriver hoping to get in front of her, to fish her out of the river or something

CYRUS: You there?

ME: i'm here

CYRUS: So we had to return to the main road and then floored it for a little while then jumped out of the truck and rushed back down to the water. We could still hear the boyfriend screaming

ME: but you got in front of her

CYRUS: The river had widened again and then there was some sort of dam, and she went over the dam before we could figure out what to do

ME: she was conscious?

CYRUS: She didn't seem to be struggling. It was kind of hard to see, or at least it's hard for me to remember. So we had to get back into the truck and drive farther down the river again—there was no other way

ME: go on

CYRUS: There was no other way

CYRUS: so on the other side of the dam there was a kind of pool—no current. And her body was there. And we rushed into the water and dragged her to the shore

ME: was she breathing

CYRUS: No

ME: so what did you

CYRUS: We laid her on the bank and I gave her or tried to give her mouth to mouth. She didn't seem, I can't really say what I mean by this, given that she wasn't breathing, but she didn't seem dead. Her white

ME: jesus, man

ME: i don't even know how to give cpr

CYRUS: shirt, her undershirt, was pulled up over her head. I had to pull it back down over her breasts. Which was somehow embarrassing. She was cut up pretty bad

CYRUS: Neither do I, really. I tried. She kind of, I don't know, threw up in my mouth

ME: you mean was revived—spit out water—so she was alive

CYRUS: No. There was vomit in her mouth I guess. And then I threw up onto the bank. She was dead

ME: jesus. i am so sorry you

CYRUS: I tried again. I didn't know what I was doing. Our teeth, I can't get this out of my mind, I accidentally clicked my teeth against her teeth at some point, like

CYRUS: like in a clumsy kiss or something. Prom. And I kept thinking of course that she had only got in the water because I had got in the water

ME: no way to blame yourself for any of this

CYRUS: And I was also worried that the cpr had killed her, I think I was pressing way too hard on her chest—or that

ME: what is jane doing during all of this

CYRUS: she would have been, at least, revived in better hands

CYRUS: I don't really know. Helping me I guess

ME: so she was dead

CYRUS: She was dead

ME: fuck, man

ME: what did you do then

CYRUS: We could hear the boyfriend screaming again. Except now I think he was injured too. He was closer. He probably got in the water again and broke an arm or leg or whatever. But he was screaming "kill me" or something from the bank. He wasn't screaming about his injuries. He knew she was dead

ME: what did you do

CYRUS: We took her body, Jane and I carried her body to the truck and raced toward the pueblo. We were maybe pretending a little to ourselves there was still something to be done, I mean, that fantasy was somewhere in our bodies—she was of course dead. But we, I mean, nobody had a phone

ME: i thought you had a cell phone

CYRUS: Broke a long time ago. So the first place we found that had people, phones, was a roadside restaurant a few minutes before the pueblo. We got out and I managed to scream out what had happened as I pointed to the body and a couple of men from the restaurant rushed out and helped us lay the body there, on the ground. Her eyes were wide open, by the way, and her mouth

ME: jesus

CYRUS: Various people gathered around, and somebody mentioned calling the police, and I guess we managed to communicate that there were others by the river—the injured boyfriend, his friend. A couple of people from the restaurant got in a car and went for them. And an old woman, she brought us some limes

ME: limes?

CYRUS: She brought us two lime wedges and said something about shock and that we should suck them and we did. Someone covered her with a blanket. I saw the pay phones and I had a calling card in the truck and I went to one of the pay phones in a daze. I think I threw up again. But I called my dad, I was desperate to ask him about the cpr, to see if I had maybe killed her or at least missed an opportunity to save her. Something like that. I wasn't

ME: you did everything you could. i'm so sorry

CYRUS: thinking clearly. And my teeth were chattering and each time they clicked I remembered her teeth

CYRUS: I did get my dad on the phone. Who knows what I sounded like. I was very confused, certainly. Sobbing. Managed to ask about the cpr, if I had done it wrong. He reassured me, although I don't remember what he said. That nothing was my fault. That she would have already choked on her vomit or something. Not that a psychiatrist knows anything about cpr. I also think he said something about my coming home

ME: none of this is in any way

CYRUS: I got off the phone and went back to the truck. One of the people who worked at the restaurant said we could go so we left

ME: your fault

ME: you didn't wait for the police?

CYRUS: Fuck no. We just left. We drove back to the apartment in total silence. We had put our clothes back over our swimsuits but were dried off from the heat by the time we got home. Like I said it was in the 80s. But my teeth were still chattering

ME: you didn't talk about what happened at all?

CYRUS: We did later. Kind of. After we showered, we both realized we hadn't eaten all day and although I felt sick I felt hungry, really hungry. We went to a little restaurant near our place we always go to. We started drinking beer and tequila which as you know I hate but which helped get this taste out of my mouth. We talked about it then

ME: what did she say

CYRUS: The taste is back, by the way

CYRUS: She was shaken up in her way. She said she wished she'd never got in the water. But she also seemed excited. Like we had had a "real" experience

ME: i guess you had

CYRUS: Yeah but I had this sense—this sense that the whole point of the trip for her—to Mexico—was for something like this, something this "real" to happen. I don't really believe that, but I felt it, and I said something about how she had got some good material for her novel

ME: is she writing a novel

CYRUS: Who knows

ME: and she responded how

CYRUS: She's probably writing a novel now

CYRUS: She was quiet. I'm sure she was angry/hurt. Then she said something about how this just is the world, that things like this happen, that one can be as cautious as one wants, can waste one's life being cautious, but that there is no avoiding the reality of death. I remember laughing at the phrase "reality of death" to show I thought it was an embarrassing cliché

ME: have you two made up

CYRUS: No. Yesterday we were both in the apartment reading and smoking but barely talked. We haven't really spoken to each other today

ME: well, you both probably just need some time, right? i mean, this would shake anybody up

ME: i am really sorry

CYRUS: Yeah

ME: about all of this

CYRUS: Thanks

CYRUS: How is Spain?

3

INSTEAD OF CONFESSING TO ISABEL THAT MY MOTHER, MY BRILLIANT and unwaveringly supportive mother, was well, that I was a liar of the most disgusting sort, I decided to imply more and more that my father, the gentlest and most generous man I knew, was a thug, a small-time fascist, El Caudillo of his household. Not only did this lie, in my view, draw Isabel's attention away from whatever discomfort she had regarding the initial dishonesty about my mom, replacing that discomfort with sympathy, but it also served to decrease my guilt; I felt much better about blaspheming both my parents, about distributing my failure as a son between them. And because this lie about my father was comically absurd, because he was the man of all the men I knew most free from any will-to-domination, it felt more like a harmless joke than a morbid tempting of fate or karmic gambling with parental health. I also felt that, in order to avoid any future confusion, I needed to get my stories straight, and so decided to replay the confession I had made to Isabel and Rufina to Teresa, who would then tell Arturo and Rafa, all of whom believed I had, when we first met, recently suffered one of life's profoundest losses. Surely some part of the mystery I liked to think I held for Teresa derived from the fact that, after my dramatic performance at the party, I made no subsequent reference to my suffering, although suffering could be read into my silences. That I was thousands of miles away from the rest of my family so soon after such a tragedy, although I never specified the timeframe, prepared the ground for my lie about my impossible father, and my new claim that I might not return to the u.s. after the completion of my fellowship furthered my image as exile. At any rate, when the rains and early dark began to give way to warmer, longer days and milder nights, and the accordion player was back in La Plaza Santa Ana and the streets were again alive, I began to see more of Teresa, who did not seem to have a job, although in theory she was employed at the gallery. I would walk to Salamanca after "working" in El Retiro and Teresa would leave the gallery in someone else's hands and accompany me to movies, bookstores, cafés.

Whenever I was with Teresa, whenever we were talking, I felt our faces engaged in a more substantial and sophisticated conversation than our voices. Her face was formidable; it seemed by turns very young and very old; when she opened her eyes wide, she looked like a child, and when she squinted in concentration, the tiny wrinkles at their outer corners made her seem worldly, wise. Because she could instantly look younger or older, more innocent or experienced than she was, she could parry whatever speech was addressed to her. If you were to accuse her, say, of reading too much into a particular scene in a movie, she would widen her eyes and look at you with an innocence that made you feel guilty of projection; if you accused her of some form of naiveté, her squint would bespeak such expanses of experience that the accusation was instantly turned back upon you. Her eyes could deflect or reflect or ironize, and then her smile, which was wide, would instantly restore a tabula rasa, benevolently forgiving any claim against her.

I believed the dialectical movement of her face, however, was challenged by our particular circumstance; I never spoke English with Teresa, not since the first night of our meeting when my volubility had swelled. I told her that this was to promote my acquisition of Spanish, but it was, in fact, to preserve the possibility of misspeaking or being misunderstood, and to secure and amplify the mystery of that inaugural outburst. I believed my rant on the way to Rafa's party had impressed her, and I was determined not to ruin it with banalities. With my performance in the car her sole sample of my English, I hoped she would always translate my fragmented Spanish in her head, transforming my halting and semicoherent utterances into the most eloquent English she could imagine. She would not, like Isabel, merely intuit depths, but would actually sound them in her painstakingly mastered second language. Of course she would never arrive at a satisfactory English formulation of whatever my Spanish negatively figured, but this would further preserve the mystique of my powers in my mother tongue. Such conversations would be the counterpoint to her ongoing work with Arturo of translating my poems, work she had almost entirely taken over; there she tried to imagine every possible Spanish correlative to my English, such as it was; here, she tried to extract from my remedial Spanish the poet's native eloquence.

As a result of these interpretations and projections, Teresa, during our conversations, was often at a loss as to what to do with her face, or at least her facial machinations were delayed; the widening and squinting of her eyes was more in response to her own internal ruminations, to what she imagined I would have said, than it was to my actual speech. I was therefore able to raise an eyebrow and communicate that I was watching Teresa attempt to translate whatever I had said, or rather, failed to say, and thus my face reclaimed from her face the powers of metacommentary. And yet as we spent more and more time together, I found myself avoiding her eyes, because when I looked at or into them, I believed I saw she saw right through me. Or I saw her see herself reflected in my eyes, saw that she knew, or was coming to know, that what interest I held for her, all of it, was virtual, that my appeal for her had little to do with my actual writing or speech, and while she was happy to let me believe she believed in my profundity, on some level she was aware that she was merely encountering herself. This anxiety was characteristic of my project's fourth phase.

One afternoon Teresa and I saw *Citizen Kane*, which was playing at El Circulo Bellas Artes, then had some chalky white wine at an adjacent sidewalk café. After making various ambiguous pronouncements about cinema, but experiencing Teresa as unusually distracted, I decided to make my confession.

"I told you before," I said slowly, "that my mother was dead. This isn't true."

"What?" she asked, suddenly interested, but not sure she'd understood.

"I told you my mom was dead, but my mom is alive," I said.

"Oh. I had assumed," she said, smiling, "that you were just drunk and high and homesick and wanted some attention." Then she leaned over and started twirling my hair and said in English, "You have a poetic license."

I blinked at her, first surprised not to feel relief, then surprised to feel an intense anger rising, as though my mother were in fact deceased and now she was calling me a liar. "I didn't want attention. I didn't have homesick," I said, my gravity cancelled by my grammar. She opened her eyes wide as I pulled away from her but said nothing, awaiting my explanation. As one part of me insisted to some other part of me that this was wonderful, a reprieve, that I could let go of my guilt and laugh about it with Teresa, I heard myself proclaim, "My mom is sick. And because——" I pretended it was difficult to go on. The smile drained quickly from her face. "I am scared . . . I was trying to imagine . . ." Her eyes grew a little wider. "I thought if I said it, I would have less fear."

"What is she sick with?" Teresa asked, which I experienced as insensitive, maybe because, while she had stopped smiling, her voice wasn't any more tender than usual, or maybe because she was interrupting my presentation. I signaled for the check, although our drinks were far from finished, then regretted signaling.

Not wanting to name a particular disease for fear of somehow condemning my mother to suffer it, I ignored the question. I reached out and touched her arm, a gesture out of character for me. "I have felt horrible about the lie. I'm sorry." Withdrawing my hand, but leaving it on the table nearly touching hers, I explained, "I came here and nobody knows me. So I thought: You can be whatever you want to people. You can say you are rich or poor. You can say you are from anywhere, that you do anything. At first I felt very free, as if my life at home wasn't real anymore." I downed my warming wine. "And I was glad to be away from my father."

While I believed the speech was working in the sense of convincing Teresa my mom was ill, or at least entreating her to suspend her disbelief, I also sensed a lack of translation, that Teresa was experiencing me as merely inarticulate. I barely resisted the temptation to wax eloquent in English, but realized my actual English was nothing compared to her image of it.

"My father," I said, "is basically a fascist."

"What do you mean by 'fascist'?" she said. Nobody, at any stage of my project, had ever asked me what I meant by "fascist" or "fascism." I felt the anger again.

"He is a man of right-wing politics," I said, meaninglessly. "He only respects violence." As I said this, I thought of my dad patiently trying to get a spider to crawl from the carpet onto a piece of paper so he could escort it safely from house to yard.

"But your mom is a feminist," she said in a voice suspiciously free of all suspicion. I'd no memory of discussing my mother's politics with Teresa.

"Yes, and publicly so is he," I said, implying everybody knew that fascists marry feminists in order to evade detection. "And what do you mean by 'feminist'?" I threw in. She just smiled ambiguously.

The check arrived. I overpaid with large euro coins, which always struck me as particularly fake, and we stood to leave; it was rare for me to pay for anything with Teresa. We walked in the direction of El Retiro. The nicotine and white wine mixed nicely with the light and still-tentative warmth and I felt confident as we walked that Teresa would give me, if nothing else, the benefit of the doubt, and I remembered, in order to buttress this belief, the time I had been stern with her at the reading and she had seemed genuinely hurt. Young women were testing their new dresses, teenagers were skateboarding in the plazas, failing again and again to land their kickflips, and we saw ourselves reflected vaguely in the silver of passing buses. I was surprised to find myself taking Teresa's hand, although I did so with the faintest trace of irony, implied, at least potentially, in the childish way I slightly swung our arms; if the intimacy were unwelcome, she would dismiss it as frivolity. At the same time I was careful to communicate, mainly with my pace, that if I was acting unburdened and optimistic it was to cover the great sadness arising from the situation with my family. I was probably aided in this representation of concealed suffering by the guilt that was beginning to spread through me, displacing nicotine and wine; it was not yet causing pain, but it was positioning itself everywhere in my body, lying in wait till evening.

We entered El Retiro through the main iron gates. It was the beginning of a long dusk and, as it was one of the first true spring evenings, people were out in force. There were young couples displaying their mutual absorption on nearly every bench, kids racing tricycles or playing tag or football, and the men who would soon be selling shaved ice were selling chipped potatoes. The voices and laughter and birds and wind and traffic combined and separated gently. As we made our way toward El Estanque, which would be full of pedal boaters, I felt that I could, in fact, imagine remaining in Spain indefinitely; I would live with and off of Teresa, my lover and translator, I would assemble a body of work, I would walk every evening through the park, I would master Spanish; a little wave of euphoria broke over me. But why was I imagining this with Teresa, not Isabel, given that I was in fact the lover of the latter, and had had no real romantic contact with the former? I had, however, so often kissed Teresa hello or good-bye, deliberately catching the corner of her mouth, or lingering near her face a second longer than necessary, that I felt we had a physical relationship, that we had been, if nothing else, in a stage of protracted courtship. But as we walked around El Estanque toward the colonnade, I was struck by the fear that this was only in my mind; Teresa must have noticed that I was catching her mouth, flirting, but surely that was not to be taken very seriously; after all, Teresa hadn't taken it seriously when I told her about the death of my mother and wept down her elegant back. I had never attempted to initiate anything with Teresa, but this was in part because I always assumed I could, that she was, if not exactly waiting for my advances, open to them, and that keeping such a possibility alive was for both of us, at least for the moment, more exciting than any consummation. While I had never thought I was in love with Teresa, whatever that might mean, I had on more than one occasion thought that she was maybe a little in love with me. And if we never slept together or otherwise "realized" our relationship, I would leave Spain with this gorgeous possibility intact, and in my memory could always ponder the relationship I might have had in the flattering light of the subjunctive. I'd never formulated this notion before, but had felt it, and only now, half an hour after our conversation at the café, was I beginning to realize my mistake; she had assumed I was lying about my mother, a goofy, drunken foreigner wanting a hug; it hardly mattered to me that her assumption was true, but it mattered to me that it mattered so little to her. When we reached the colonnade, we sat on the cool steps not far from a circle of drummers and she began to roll a spliff. I looked at her and she was aureate in the failing light and humming something to go with the drums and the prospect of her not being at least a little in love with me was crushing.

I wanted to kiss her or say something dramatic in English, but I knew I would make myself ridiculous. Instead, as we finished smoking, I pretended to remember with a start:

"I have to meet someone," I said, standing with a suddenness that declared the someone important.

"o.k.," she said, her face registering no curiosity, let alone jealousy. I hoped against hope this was affectation. "Soon we should talk about the new translations," she said. The gallery was going to print a small bilingual pamphlet of my poems.

"Claro," I said, and kissed her twice quickly far from the mouth and walked hurriedly back the way we'd come. Without paying attention to where I was going, I retraced our steps and found myself, cold and sober, back in front of El Circulo de Bellas Artes. I bought a ticket for the next show, which I thought was *Campanadas a*

medianoche. I sat in the same seat, Teresa's absence beside me. I took a
yellow pill and waited; I was half an hour early. I drifted off, but was
awakened by the movie's opening strains: it was the second showing
of *Citizen Kane*.

————

Isabel and I were smoking in bed in the early evening and she was reading Ana María Matute and I was reading Tolstoy's *The Kreutzer Sonata*
when I mentioned apropos of nothing that I would like to see Granada
at some point and she said there was a night train that took about five
hours so we packed what we could in the bags we always carried and
walked to Atocha; I bought our tickets. We killed an hour drinking
coffee in the atrium and then we boarded the archaic-looking Talgo
train and found our seats and opened our respective books again, looking up at each other when with a jerk the train began to move.

Excepting subways, a few commuter trains, and the miniature
train in a Topeka park, I had never traveled by rail, as archaic a method
of conveyance, I thought to myself, as poetry; a few minutes later I
offered this thought to Isabel. She laughed and leaned over and kissed
me and I wished that Teresa could see us, dark fields sliding by. Isabel
removed the silver sticks from her hair and leaned her head against
my shoulder and drifted off while I flipped through the Tolstoy for a
half-remembered passage about a train, but couldn't find it. It didn't
matter; every sentence, regardless of its subject, became mimetic of
the action of the train, and the train mimetic of the sentence, and I felt
suddenly coeval with its syntax. Because the sentences of Tolstoy, or
rather Constance Garnett's translations of Tolstoy, were in perfect
harmony with the motion of the Talgo, real time and the time of
prose began to merge, and reading, instead of removing me from the
world, intensified my experience of the present.

wn the book and began to think: this strange experience of the sense of harmony between the rhythms of a reproduc-d the real, their structural identity, so that the subject of the sentence was precisely the time of its being furthered—this was what I valued in one of the only people I described as a "major poet" without irony, John Ashbery. I fished his *Selected Poems* from my bag, careful not to disturb Isabel, and opened it at random and read a little. Here also one could experience the texture of time as it passed, a shadow train, life's white machine. Ashbery's flowing sentences always felt as if they were making sense, but when you looked up from the page, it was impossible to say what sense had been made; while they used the language of logical connection—"but," "therefore," "so"—and the language that implied narrative development—"then," "next," "later"—such terms were merely propulsive; there was no actual organizing logic or progression. Reading an Ashbery sentence, an elaborate sentence stretched over many lines, one felt the arc and feel of thinking in the absence of thoughts. His pronouns—"it," "you," "we," "I"—created a sense of intimacy, as though you were being addressed or doing the addressing or were familiar with the context the poem assumed, but you could never be sure of their antecedents, person or thing. The "it" in an Ashbery poem seemed ultimately to refer to the mysteries of the poem itself; in the absence of any stable external referent, the poem's procedures invested its pronouns, and the "you" devolved upon the reader. I read:

> As long as it is there
> You will desire it as its tag of wall sinks
> Deeper as though hollowed by sunlight that
> Just fits over it; it is both mirage and the little
> That was present, the miserable totality
> Mustered at any given moment, like your eyes

> *And all they speak of, such as your hands, in lost*
> *Accents beyond any dream of ever wanting them again.*
> *To have this to be constantly coming back from—*
> *Nothing more, really, than surprise at your absence*
> *And preparing to continue the dialogue into*
> *Those mysterious and near regions that are*
> *Precisely the time of its being furthered.*

The best Ashbery poems, I thought, although not in these words, describe what it's like to read an Ashbery poem; his poems refer to how their reference evanesces. And when you read about your reading in the time of your reading, mediacy is experienced immediately. It is as though the actual Ashbery poem were concealed from you, written on the other side of a mirrored surface, and you saw only the reflection of your reading. But by reflecting your reading, Ashbery's poems allow you to attend to your attention, to experience your experience, thereby enabling a strange kind of presence. But it is a presence that keeps the virtual possibilities of poetry intact because the true poem remains beyond you, inscribed on the far side of the mirror: "You have it but you don't have it. / You miss it, it misses you. / You miss each other."

Isabel shifted and I put the book away and leaned my head against the mass of her hair and fell asleep. We were both awakened when the train stopped, still a few hours from Granada. We stepped off the train and smoked in the dark, although you could smoke on the train; the night air was cool, laced with jasmine, if they have that in Spain. Isabel described a dream I couldn't understand. The train made a noise that indicated it was preparing to leave and we went back to our seats, fell asleep again, then were both gently roused by a conductor, who said we were approaching Granada, last stop. It was a slightly lighter dark now that dawn was an hour away and when the train pulled into the station and eventually halted we disembarked and wandered out of the station in a state of not unpleasant fatigue.

We found a cab and drove to a hotel Isabel knew in the Albaicín, a neighborhood of impossibly narrow, winding streets on a hill facing the Alhambra. The hotel was surprisingly nice given the rates; Moorish medieval architecture, intricate woodwork, and a courtyard with a green mosaic. We were led to a simple room with exposed beams, a room for that reason reminiscent of my apartment, and we slept through the morning. When I woke I was for a moment unsure of my surroundings, then remembered the spontaneous trip, the train, and again wished Teresa could see me interleaved with Isabel, her jet hair splayed against the heavily starched sheets. We showered, dressed, and walked into the preternaturally bright day, wandering the threadlike streets until we found a sidewalk café, although there wasn't much sidewalk, where we ordered orange juice, croissants, coffee. From the café you could see the Alhambra on a vast and hilly terrace across the river. Isabel was wearing her hair down and looked beautiful to me and I told her so. I paid and we descended into the city and visited the cathedral and a small modern art museum where I pretended to take copious notes.

When we were ready to eat again it was late afternoon and we returned to the Albaicín to find a restaurant Isabel knew. Within a few minutes of our arrival we were presented with giant plates of fried fish and squid that either Isabel had ordered without my knowing or that were the restaurant's only dish. They also brought us a bottle of nearly frozen white wine and I drank several glasses quickly and felt immediately and pleasantly drunk. I said something to Isabel about the experience of braided temporalities in ancient cities and she nodded in a way that showed she wasn't listening.

"What are you thinking about?" I asked her, refilling both of our glasses, the bottle almost empty.

She hesitated. "We never talk about our relationship, about the rules," she said. I always thought the rule was that we wouldn't. This was the first time I'd heard her refer to our "relationship" at all. I knew what was coming: she wanted to assure herself I wasn't seeing anybody else, that at least for as long as I was in Spain, I was hers exclusively. Maybe she also wanted to know how long I planned to stay, if I was seriously considering remaining in Spain after my fellowship.

"I am in a relationship," was the English equivalent of what she said. I felt the wind had been knocked out of me. I smiled to imply that of course we both had other relationships.

"He must have an open mind," I said, holding the smile, "to allow you to travel with other men." I was surprised to feel devastated.

"He has been working in Barcelona this year. He was here at Christmas and a couple of other times. He'll be back in Madrid starting in June." The way she said "June" hinted she would like to know where I planned to be then. I remembered I hadn't seen Isabel much around the holidays.

I pushed my plate away a little and lit a cigarette. "So what happens to us in June?" Now the seafood looked alien, arachnoid, repulsive.

She smiled in a way that said, "I really like you, we've had a lot of fun, but in June our time is up." Then she said, "I don't know."

"What's his name?" I asked, suggesting with my tone that whatever his name was, I thought he was a harmless little boy.

"Oscar," she said, and her voice declared he was a man among men. "We decided to break up when he had to move to Barcelona for work. Or to at least be open to other people. But now we both feel that we should be together when he returns." In English I thought "Oscar" sounded silly; in Spanish: very serious.

I had let the smile slip away. "Does he know about me?" I felt like crying. I tried to long for Teresa, but could not.

"We've both been seeing other people. We don't ask each other about it," she said. I wondered how many other people she had been with recently. "Just like you and I don't ask each other," she added. It was clear she *hoped* I had other relationships.

"Claro," I said, recomposing my smile to indicate I'd slept with half the women in Madrid. "You love him?" It was a stupid, clichéd question.

"Yes," she said, her tone confirming it was a stupid, clichéd question.

"Well," I said, "there is still some time before June." I imagined breaking the bottle over her head then raking my throat with the jagged glass.

"Yes," she said, and leaned over and kissed me. "There is a lot of time before you go back."

"I didn't say I was going back," I said, flatly.

"But your mom," she said.

I was grateful for a reason to be upset. "I don't want to talk about my mother with you." Then, after a pause: "I have to piss." I went to the bathroom and splashed water on my face and looked in the mirror and let out a single ridiculous sob. Then I laughed at myself, applied some more water, dried off my face, and returned to the table, sad but stabilized. "Sorry," I said. "It can be hard to think about my mom."

"Of course," she said, "I'm sorry." I kissed her to assert my spirits were ultimately unaffected by our talk and resumed my increasingly fragmented and incoherent speech about time in ancient cities. She seemed interested now, although I suspected it was charity.

We left the restaurant and walked back down through the Albaicín into the center of the city. Isabel put her arm around me in gesture that expressed less affection than relief at having clarified things between us. As we walked and dusk began to fall and Isabel wrapped herself in a shawl, I thought back to the scene at the lake when Miguel hit me; that was probably around the time she'd broken up with Oscar. And who knew if Rufina's suspicion of me was the issue of her disdain for Oscar or her affection for him. We sat on a bench in a little plaza and watched the goatsuckers spar. My mind was revising many months' worth of assumptions; I felt something like a physical change as my recent past liquefied and reformed. What was left of the light burnished what it touched; Isabel was half shadow and half bronze, boundless and bounded. We got high.

When it was unmistakably night we walked down toward and then along the Darro; there was some sort of small festival and part of the river was illumined by torches. Little kids dressed in white, glowing softly, darted through the streets. It had been a while since either of us had spoken, and whereas for months I had imagined Isabel's silences as devoted to me entirely, I was now unsure if I was even in her thoughts.

"When I am near a river," I heard myself say, "I think of my time in Mexico."

"When were you in Mexico?" she asked.

"I spent some time with my girlfriend in a town called Xalapa before I came to Spain." I paused to suggest she might still be my girlfriend. "We went on a trip one weekend. We found a place to swim. There was a violent current, but we decided to swim anyway. There was another man. He wanted his girlfriend to swim. But she was afraid of the current. In the end she entered the river." I paused again, lighting a cigarette. Why was my Spanish so halting? "She did not know how to swim. She had bad luck and the current carried her. We followed her. We found her body in the river. I gave her"——

here I touched my mouth and then gestured toward Isabel's—"to make her breathe. But it was too late. We took her body to a place with phones. We called the police. An old woman gave us limes."

"Limes," Isabel confirmed.

"She gave us limes for sucking because we suffered shock."

"My God," Isabel said, and took my hand. I wanted her to ask about my girlfriend, I was preparing a speech about Jane, but she didn't. We sat down on the low stone wall that ran along the river and watched the reflections of the torches in the water and after a while Isabel began to talk. First she described a house or home or apartment, a description vaguely familiar from her first speech at the lake, but I was still unsure if her words attached to a household or the literal structure where she lived. I could understand more now than then; my Spanish had, despite myself, significantly improved, but this fact itself got in the way of understanding: I was measuring the time that had elapsed since the night at the lake by virtue of my increased comprehension, but this attention to the quality of my own attention crowded out Isabel's meaning. Eventually I shook free of my self-absorption and came to grasp what she was saying, aided by how slowly she was speaking. That summer her brother died—she referred to his death as if we'd discussed it before—and she was looking through his stuff, records and books, deciding what to take with her when the family moved, she had found a notebook, a notebook from school, what grade she wasn't sure, and it had numbers written all over its pages: 1066, 312, 1936, 1492, 800, 1776, etc. At first she didn't know what these were, didn't recognize them as years, significant years he probably had to memorize for a history test, and so had written the numbers again and again, filling an entire notebook with them, and she convinced herself that it was an elaborate coded message, a message to her. She must

have known, she was sixteen, that this was impossible, but she had
let herself be convinced, and the notebook became her most trea-
sured possession. She never attempted to decipher the code, the
point was not to read the message; the point was that there was an
ongoing conversation between her and her brother, an uncon-
cluded correspondence. A few months before Oscar left for
Barcelona he found the notebook, which Isabel had never mentioned to anybody, although she hadn't really hidden it either,
keeping it in a box with various childhood possessions on the top
shelf of her closet. It suddenly occurred to me that we never went
to Isabel's apartment not only because my apartment had more
privacy but also because she probably wanted to keep me away
from her roommates and/or reserve her bed for Oscar exclusively.
Oscar asked why she had this notebook with years written all over
it and this was the first time she let herself realize they were in fact
just years. She was furious at Oscar for destroying her fantasy and
screamed at him and then burst into tears and then told him the
whole story and cried and cried as though only then, many years
after the accident, did she fully confront the reality of her brother's
death. They sat on the bed together carefully turning the pages
and Isabel wept and ran her fingers over the years, which were
written in blue and red.

Later, when Oscar and Isabel broke up or at least agreed to see
other people because he was leaving for Barcelona, Isabel had fallen
apart, and had somehow felt her brother's death was upon her
again, because Oscar was the only person she talked to about her
brother, and because of the scene they shared with the notebook.
One thing she loved about me, she said, and it was clear she meant
"loved" in the weakest sense, was that I never asked her questions
about her brother after she talked to me about him at the lake.

I said nothing. After a while we resumed our walk and wandered back up into the Albaicín and found our hotel. It was a steep walk and we were tired by the time we arrived. There were a few tables in the courtyard and I asked the teenager who was sweeping up if it was possible to have wine. He brought us a warm, unlabeled bottle of white wine and two tall glasses filled with ice. We drank and smoked until the bottle was empty and then went to our room and fucked quickly and I felt completely in love. Isabel went to sleep and I opened the tall wooden shutters and leaned out overlooking the street and smoked. There were no cars parked on the street and it was perfectly quiet and I thought it probably looked like this in 1066, 312, 1936, whatever. Then I thought it probably didn't, got in bed, and fell asleep.

The next morning we had breakfast at the same café and I said to Isabel that the more I thought about it the more eager I was to get back as I had to work with someone named Teresa on a pamphlet of my poetry that was to be published. I said this as if I were nervous about saying anything regarding Teresa in front of Isabel, nervous I might hurt her feelings.

"We can take the train tonight," Isabel said, and because she didn't seem jealous I was furious.

"Let's just go back now," I said, which was ridiculous.

"Now? You haven't seen the Alhambra," she said.

"I've seen it before," I lied. Now she looked jealous. I was elated.

"With whom?" she asked, and it was clear she was only pretending not to care.

"Teresa," I said, and then pretended I wished I hadn't. "And her brother."

"When?" she asked.

"Around Christmas," I said. I had the sense that Isabel wanted to be my only guide, that while she didn't care who I slept with, she didn't want another woman showing me the architectural wonders of Spain.

"But you said you wanted to see Granada—that's why we came," she said, remembering our conversation in bed.

"I did want to see it again," I said. "And I'll come back again."

"Fine," she said, angry. I wondered if I would be the only American in history who visited Granada without seeing the Alhambra.

After breakfast we took a cab to the train station, bought our tickets, and had around an hour and a half to kill before the Talgo left. It wasn't until we actually bought our tickets that I realized the last thing I wanted to do was to go back. We found a café and ordered more coffee and the caffeine along with Isabel's jealousy inspired me to say, "Look, when we get back to Madrid, let's just stay one night. I can get my work done and we can pack for a longer trip. Then we can take another train to Galicia or Lisbon or wherever."

Isabel smiled at me, having gone at an alarming rate from anger to something more like pity. "I can't," she said. "I have to work."

"Take vacation," I said.

"I can't," she repeated softly, as if I'd asked her to marry me. "Don't you have work too?" There was gentle derision in the question. For the first time, I took a joke about poetry personally.

"Is your work more important?" I asked, as if her work were guarding paintings.

"No," she said simply. I was crushed by how easily she ignored my implication.

We spent the rest of our downtime at the café, then boarded the train, and passed the next five hours reading, napping, smoking, but almost never speaking. I missed my parents terribly. By day the Spanish countryside looked a lot like Kansas.

Late in the fourth phase of my project I decided to up the dosage, to take two white pills each morning instead of one. I had enough; before leaving the u.s. I had been given a year's supply, which required a special letter from my doctor, and earned me strange looks from the pharmacist, and I had already had a month's worth of medication on hand before acquiring the stockpile, which I had then divided into several small bottles. Besides, I could always see a psychiatrist in Spain—if, for instance, I stayed after my fellowship, maybe teaching English. Or I could just stop taking the white pills when I ran out; I wasn't really convinced they did much for me in the first place. When I began taking them, I had a very pleasant insomnia, reading until dawn without fatigue; that was the only significant side effect and it passed with regrettable speed. After that, I was never sure what, if any, effect they had; I'd considered going off them at various points, but each time I hesitated, wondering if in fact they were buoying me; maybe my lows would be much lower, insufferably lower, without them.

The white pills certainly did not seem to work for me the way they worked for some people; I always felt a few strains of rumination away from full orchestral panic, I was almost always acutely aware of the bones beneath the face. But then I drank and smoked in a way that made tracking the specific effects of the white pills difficult. The ritual of taking them, however, had become important to me, not because of some possible placebo effect, where the mere fact of ingestion steadied me, but rather because they were a daily reminder that I was officially fucked up, that I was undergoing treatment, that I had a named condition. It was a Eucharistic rite of self-abnegation in which I acknowledged to myself that I was incapable of facing the world without designer medication and thereby absolved myself of some portion of my agency; it was a little humiliating, a little liberating.

When I got back from Granada I began to spiral, not out of control, but downward, nevertheless, in a helix of small pitch. I had not realized how much I was invested in the idea that Isabel and Teresa were invested in me, and now that it seemed neither had the inclination even to feign serious investment, I felt not only rejected, but as though many months of research had evaporated. It occurred to me that I could at least feel less guilty regarding all the lies about my family, as nothing significant had been built upon them, but in fact I felt wave after wave of intensified remorse. It became increasingly clear to me that I would have to confess my slander to my parents at some point in order not to be consumed by it, which added dread to my guilt. My distress about Isabel and Teresa, coupled with my guilt about my parents, opened onto larger questions about my fraudulence; that I *was* a fraud had never been in question—who wasn't? Who wasn't squatting in one of the handful of prefabricated subject positions proffered by capital or whatever you wanted to call it, lying every time she said "I"; who wasn't a bit player in a looped infomercial for the damaged life? If I was a poet, I had become one because poetry, more intensely than any other practice, could not evade its anachronism and marginality and so constituted a kind of acknowledgment of my own preposterousness, admitting my bad faith in good faith, so to speak. I could lie about my interest in the literary response to war because by making a mockery of the notion that literature could be commensurate with mass murder I was not defaming the victims of the latter, but the dilettantes of the former, rejecting the political claims repeatedly made by the so-called left for a poetry radical only in its unpopularity. I had been a small-time performance artist pretending to be a poet, but now, with an alarming fervor, I wanted to write great poems. I wanted my "work" to take on the United States of Bush, to shed its scare quotes, and I wanted, after I self-immolated on the Capitol steps or whatever, to become the Miguel Hernández of late empire, for Isabel and Teresa and everybody everywhere to read my poems, shatter storefronts, etc. This was a structure of feeling, not an idea, which made it harder to dismiss, and I felt it more intensely in direct proportion to its ridiculousness. And when I doubled my dosage, and the insomnia returned, I began to read and write feverishly. This was less a new faith in poetry than a sudden loss of faith in pure potentiality.

Besides the insomnia, which this time lasted, save for a few nights of long and total and dreamless sleep, for a couple of weeks, I experienced two other notable side effects: first, my jaw was constantly and involuntarily clenched; second, I had what the internet told me was sexual anhedonia, lovely phrase. Both side effects had a certain rightness of fit with my general despondency, which was not diminishing, and I found this correspondence comforting, the way one savors abysmal weather when one feels abysmal. Additionally, I began to convince myself that the white pills were responsible for the intensity of my suffering, that I was having an adverse reaction, and this mitigated my fear of feeling that way forever; if I went off the white pills, I'd feel better. But I was too scared to test this hypothesis, and so, after a few days, I upped my dosage even further, taking a third white pill each morning, and when, after reading or revising poems for several hours, I would suddenly start crying, burying my face in a towel so the neighbors wouldn't hear, or, when shopping for wine or cigarettes or hash, I felt mild dissociation, the world curling at its edges, I would reassure myself by saying that the white pills were themselves the primary cause.

The relationship I might have had in the flattering light of the subjunctive.

After the first week of my new dosage, however, a week in which neither Isabel nor Teresa called on me, I achieved a new emotional state, or a state in which emotions no longer obtained. When I would try to describe this condition in chats with Cyrus it seemed utterly contradictory; on the one hand, I now felt nothing, my affect a flat spectrum over a defined band; I could watch videos of beheadings or contractors firing on Iraqi civilians or the Fox News commentators without a reaction and I did. I reread Levin's most soul-wrenching scenes without the slightest affective fluctuation. Although I still did not leave my apartment because I was waiting for Isabel and/or Teresa to ring my bell and run up the stairs and confess her love for me, begging me to remain in Spain or to take her with me to the States, I waited now without feeling. And if one of them were to appear and make the most dramatic spectacle of her affection, I began to doubt I'd be moved significantly. At the same time, however, I felt a kind of euphoria at my sudden inability to feel, an exaggerated second order of feeling that did not alter the first order numbness. This euphoria, if that's what it was, was very far from my body, and there-fore compatible with my anhedonia; it was as if I were suspended in a warm bath outside of myself. I felt something like a rush of power, the power to experience the world as though under glass, and this detachment, coupled with my reduced need or capacity for sleep, gave me a kind of vampiric energy, although I was my own prey. I could read and write for hours on end with what felt like total con-centration, barely noticing nightfall, and in the early hours of the morning, I would wander around Madrid, passing Isabel's apartment or Teresa's gallery just to show myself I could do so without a spike in agony. I would often watch the dawn from the colonnade in El Retiro or one of the benches on El Paseo del Prado or take the Metro to a stop I didn't know and watch the sunrise there, return home, sleep for a few hours, wake and take white pills, hash, coffee, and with an uncanny energy resume my adventures in insensitivity. I was vaguely afraid, of what I couldn't say; maybe that I would throw myself in front of a bus without knowing what I was doing or break into Isabel's apartment and tear apart her brother's notebook or put a trash can through the gallery window or otherwise act out, pow-erless to stop myself from such a distance. But I also felt, for the first time, like a writer, as if all the real living were on the page, and I had to purchase a stack of ruled notebooks from Casa del Libro to con-tain my poems and notes. I told myself I was going to write new poems of such beauty and significance that when Teresa translated and printed them and I gave a copy to Isabel, both women would realize that they had been in the presence of a poet who alone was able to array the fallen materials of the real into a song that tran-scended it.

Finally, Isabel came. It was late afternoon and I was reading "The Waste Land" online, stealing phrases. She said something about my apartment being dirty and arranged a few things and it was clear to me that all she felt for me was pity, convinced, no doubt, that she had broken my heart. After saying something about her work that I didn't try to understand, she told me she was going to Barcelona, probably in the next few days, and would stay with Oscar until they both returned. I experienced the shape of pain but no pain, and said that while it was a shame I wouldn't see her more, that I was going to miss her terribly, I wished her and Oscar all the best; indeed, if I stayed in Madrid beyond my fellowship, maybe we could all have a drink together at some point, although I understood if that would be difficult for *him*. My Spanish had never sounded so fluent. I heard myself saying that before she left I'd at least like to take her to dinner, drinks. She had probably planned not to see me again after this visit to my apartment, had imagined a difficult scene, but now that I was showing myself more or less indifferent to her departure, and capable of almost alarming lightness, she said yes, sure, that would be great. I told her for some reason that I was busy that night but that if she came by the next evening around nine we would have our good-bye celebration. She kissed me on the cheek, said how sweet I was, and left. After a momentary flash of anger, I felt nothing.

A few hours after Isabel's visit I walked to the gallery, a half-hour walk, smoking and reciting some of my poems to myself, barely feeling the ground beneath me. It was a warm evening, or I was oblivious to the cold, and the streetlights and shop windows and lights of passing cars were intensely bright; the conversation of pedestrians and the sound of traffic and music from passing cars was intensely loud; I wondered if these were side effects. Teresa wasn't there, but Arturo was, and appeared very happy to see me. I told him I had been in Granada with someone named Isabel and he smiled at me but asked no questions. Maybe his expression implied

Teresa would be jealous. He asked me about my poems and I took four notebooks out of my bag and gave them to him and explained they were just from this week and I wondered which were his favorite poems and if there were any they wanted to include in the pamphlet. He seemed genuinely excited, and I thought to myself that that was both touching and somehow sad, but felt neither touched nor saddened. He said I must come to the opening on Friday for the show of several well-known Spanish painters and he added, maybe significantly, that Teresa would be eager to see me; I said fine. Then for some reason I embraced and kissed Arturo with an ambiguous passion I didn't feel and walked home. For the first time in many days I was tired and quickly fell asleep.

When I awoke it was a little after three in the morning and I was perhaps hungrier than I had ever been. I'd been eating very little for two weeks, and the return of my appetite, I assumed, represented a shift in my body's relation to the white pills. I ate an entire two-day-old baguette and as I ate I checked my e-mail and there was a message in English from Teresa, who had only e-mailed me once or twice in the past, saying that she had heard I was back from "traveling with Isabel" and that she missed me. I felt a small, distant thrill, further confirmation that my body had acclimated a little to the drugs, or that the drugs were already losing their effectiveness, and I went easily back to sleep and slept until the early afternoon.

After I showered, I went to a jeweler near my apartment and with my parents' credit card, which I was only to use in emergencies, bought Isabel a hundred-and-fifty-euro silver necklace. It was the first time I'd used the card and it was by far the most expensive gift I'd ever purchased. I asked the handsome woman who sold me the necklace where I should take my girlfriend for dinner as it was our anniversary, what did she consider the nicest restaurant in Madrid, the fancier the better, given the occasion. She said she liked Zalacaín, but that it was probably difficult to get in. Smiling, I asked if I could use her phone to call them and beg. She said of course and I called and they said they could, owing to a cancellation, seat two that night at nine thirty. I thanked them and the woman gift wrapped the necklace and said something about how lucky my girlfriend was as I left.

I went to the Corte Inglés and bought a dress shirt, a stylish-looking knockoff black suit that they could tailor within the hour, and a pair of Spanish shoes. It all cost a few hundred euros and again I used the card. I went home and took a second shower, rolled and smoked a spliff, read the Quixote for a while, and then put on the suit. When Isabel arrived she seemed impressed by my appearance; I felt handsome, not, as I had expected, ridiculous. After she considered me for a while, Isabel said her own clothes weren't elegant enough; she hadn't thought we were going anywhere so formal. I said we were going to Zalacaín as though I went there all the time and she said she had heard of it but would have to go change. I told her there wasn't time, although there was, and that she looked beautiful, which she did, but I said she looked beautiful with some condescension, as if I doubted she owned sufficiently elegant clothing. We took a cab and were early to Zalacaín and Isabel was visibly underdressed; people were staring at the scarf in her hair and the hostess hesitated before asking for my name. Isabel was too attractive for her casual attire to cause much of a scandal, but I smiled apologetically at the hostess, who smiled back at me as I gave her my name; I could feel Isabel blushing.

It turned out our table was ready and we were seated and I said to the waiter that my Spanish wasn't good enough to order so I asked that he just bring us whatever the chef recommended, along with a bottle of his favorite Spanish white; my manner suggested I had made this request in several European capitals and languages. When

I heard myself ask for a Spanish wine, which, no matter how expensive, would be several orders of magnitude cheaper than the others, I realized I was not entirely out of my mind, which meant I should stop acting as if I were: I was on track to spend more in one day than I'd spent in the previous two months including rent, and all of it in a manner entirely visible to my parents. How would my ailing mom and fascist dad respond to such acting out was the joke I made to myself; I heard my laughter in my head and it sounded foreign.

Isabel and I had nothing to say. She was nervous, angry, confused; she didn't drink the aperitifs they brought us on a silver tray. I drank both of them in a manner that communicated I was entirely prepared to make a scene, whatever scene Isabel might like. But worried she would just stand up and leave, I asked her as though there were no tension in the air if she'd had to quit her job at the language school. She said she hadn't and I realized she'd told me this already. I told her I was sorry about my insisting on such an abrupt return from Granada. She said it was fine and asked after my poems, how work on the little book was coming. I said good, great in fact, that I had never written so much, and I imagined I saw a spark of interest in Isabel as she perhaps remembered my notes and pondered the possibility that she was, in one way or another, involved in them. I told her I would send her a copy in a tone designed to demolish this fantasy if she had it, my voice suggesting I wouldn't even remember her by the time the book came out, but her smile made it clear this was not a believable implication, that I was trying too hard to appear indifferent. I softened a little, felt myself sink into my chair, and for a second I feared I might let out the same sob, a sob very close to awkward laughter, that I'd released in Granada. Wine was served for me to taste and, making a face that expressed mild disappointment, a face I often made while reading, I said that it was fine.

A plate of steak tartare was brought to us and Isabel looked at it with muffled surprise and it was clear she had never imagined eating finely chopped raw beef. I asked her how Rufina was as I served her a punishingly large portion and it was suddenly obvious, much more obvious than I intended, that my clothes and the expensive meal were saying to Isabel: of course I never took our relationship seriously; I am a fabulously wealthy American from the United States of Bush, I have merely been acquiring experience, slumming, etc. I felt a wave of guilt and wanted to apologize and worried, having felt a wave of anything, that I was headed for a precipice. I could barely make myself eat. Isabel didn't respond to my question, but I had the sense that, if she were embarrassed, it was only on my behalf.

Plates were taken away and new ones arrived; Isabel appeared relieved by the familiarity of the artichokes and asparagus wrapped in bacon; I couldn't taste anything. I was moving at inappropriate speed through the wine. I asked what Oscar was doing in Barcelona and she said either that he was a mechanic or was being retrained for something mechanical or that he sold cars or worked for a car company; I didn't care. I asked what he looked like and she put her hand on my hand and said let's not talk about Oscar, let this be our night. I smiled at her and tried to look relaxed but when the next dish was brought, something involving caviar and maybe quail eggs, I thought that I might vomit. I could not attempt a bite and my face felt hot and I could barely drink the wine, but did. I must have looked terrible; Isabel asked if I was all right. In my head I said no, my mom just died, and I laughed aloud and my laugh was aberrant. I said that I was fine, but as I said it, I realized for the first time that I was without my yellow pills; I couldn't have brought my bag to such a restaurant and hadn't thought to transfer the yellow pills to my jacket pocket because in the last week of my protracted neuropathy

I hadn't taken any. Still, I reached into the jacket pocket and felt the necklace in its case and began to panic; I was respiring no oxygen when I inhaled; it was like trying to drink through a straw with many holes. I said excuse me, stood on very weak legs, the floor uneven now, and walked to the bathroom, which was as lavish as everything else and smelled like roses. I splashed water on my face and told myself, aloud, to calm down, and for a second I felt better, that this would pass, and then I noticed for the first time that there was an attendant in the bathroom, which again made me feel crazy. The chemical taste I often experienced after panic was already in my mouth, an ominous sign; I spat in the sink despite the attendant, rinsed, but the taste intensified. I felt another wave of nausea and went into a stall and vomited. For a moment it occurred to me that I might be having a medical emergency; if I died, blood tests would reveal to my family that, as the saying goes, drugs were involved. The blood tests, the credit card bill, the notebooks filled with incomprehensible poems—had I tried to kill myself without my knowledge, were those so many suicide notes? I sat on the toilet with my head in my hands and cried as quietly as possible. Fortunately, the crying helped. Eventually I stopped heaving, left the stall, and again splashed water on my face. The attendant asked me if I was all right. I blinked at him, breathed deeply, mumbled something about my family, and deposited a handful of coins in the bowl beside him, which might have been for mints.

I felt much better now, that is, I felt next to nothing as I returned to the table where Isabel awaited me with genuine concern. I said I was sorry, that I'd had a dizzy spell, but it had passed, and I drank my wine and felt restored. I wasn't sure how long I'd been gone but the table had been cleared and soon we were served lamb and something involving lobster along with a new bottle of red wine the waiter explained was related to the white. I wasn't hungry but I was no longer repulsed by the food and as I ate a little I asked Isabel what she wanted to do after dinner. She said she didn't know and I said that we could do anything she wanted. She thought for a while and smiled and said that she had never spent the night at a fancy hotel. I heard myself say we would stay in the Ritz-Carlton directly opposite the Prado. As I drank more I could eat more and as I grew drunker the money became increasingly unreal. This was accompanied by a wave of benevolence that I directed at Isabel, and I began to speak to her in a Spanish that sounded, at least to me, impeccable.

"I have been upset since we talked about Oscar. When you told me about him, I realized how much I cared about you, and it's very hard to know that I won't be able to see you again," I said.

"Yes," she said, without malice, "but what does it mean that you only realized how much you cared when you heard about Oscar?"

"I didn't mean that exactly, but it's difficult to express myself with subtlety in Spanish," I said.

"You are fluent in Spanish, Adán," she said, maybe sadly.

"I was angry and jealous and hurt and acting like a teenager," I ignored her. "But now I just want to tell you how wonderful it's been to spend time with you, how wonderful I think you are, and how, while it's painful for me that you'll be with someone else, I wish you only the best." I started to reach for my glass to toast her but then thought that would be ridiculous.

She opened her mouth, but hesitated before speaking, and for some reason it suddenly occurred to me: there is no Oscar. Oscar was a test, it was revenge for my insisting on having a separate social life, for the reading in Salamanca. It was a trap to move me toward some kind of commitment. I was waiting for my emotional response to this revelation to declare itself when she refuted it: "You are very sweet. I will always love you." Her tone made it clear that she loved a lot of people in a lot of ways.

Two men cleared our plates and scraped the tablecloth and gave me a dessert menu that I handed to Isabel and I asked if they had half bottles of champagne; they did, I ordered one, and Isabel asked me what I wanted for dessert. I wondered if she'd ever had crème brûlée. She said she hadn't so we ordered it and they brought chocolate-covered strawberries compliments of the chef with our champagne. I began to make fun of the waiters' seriousness and Isabel found it hilarious; we were laughing loudly, attracting glances. We had a few bites of the dessert and finished the champagne and were by then quite drunk. I did not look at the check when it came. The waiter returned my card, I signed the receipt, and left a large tip in cash, probably a faux pas.

They called us a cab and we stumbled into it and I asked for the Ritz, the very name of which struck us both as hysterical, and we made out for the length of the ride. I paid and we went into the hotel and I spoke to the receptionist in English.

"I'm just in from New York and need a room for the night," I said, as if the words "New York" explained everything. Isabel seemed impressed by my English.

The receptionist typed on a computer and said, "We have available to you sir a classic room with a king bed and a balcony."

"Remind me how much those rooms are," I said, my eyebrows suggesting I was only curious how these rates compared to New York, Milan, Paris.

"They are three hundred and ninety euros per night sir," she said.

I considered telling Isabel that no rooms were available, but even without English, she would discern it was a lie. "O.K.," I said, thinking of my apartment two hundred yards away; my rent was three hundred and seventy-five euros a month.

I asked if I could pay in advance and did. The receptionist began to say something about luggage, then coughed her way out of it. A bellboy, if that's the word, led us to our room, which was as fancy as the restaurant, and I asked him in English if he would bring us a bottle of the cheapest white wine they had; he said of course, but refused to return my conspiratorial smile. Isabel slipped off her shoes and opened the windows and said she was going to take a shower. The wine was there by the time she came out of the bathroom wearing one of the hotel's plush white robes; we drank, made love, and then smoked near the window. I ordered another bottle, my affectedly formal manner on the phone uproarious to Isabel. Then we made love again and smoked again, Isabel now drunker than I'd ever seen her; she held my head in her hands, mumbling something I couldn't understand, barely Spanish. Finally she passed out and I stood alone at the window, the room dark, and looked across the street at the Prado. I thought of the great artist for a while.

4

I WOKE UP IN THE FIFTH PHASE OF MY PROJECT AS IF IN RESPONSE TO a loud noise. Isabel was still sleeping, maybe because of all the wine. I got out of bed, dressed, splashed water on my face, brushed my teeth with the complimentary brush, gargled the designer mouthwash, and smoked a cigarette near the window. It was still early, rush hour. A few fire trucks passed by on El Paseo del Prado, sirens blaring. I was hungover, disoriented. Then several police cars passed. I leaned out the window and looked down the street, but couldn't see anything. I told Isabel I'd be back soon; she shifted in her sleep as I left the room. I took the elevator to the lobby where people were huddled around TVs. I asked the bellboy in English what happened but he was distracted by other guests; I left the hotel and walked into the sun. Or was it cloudy?

Now trucks full of what looked like soldiers or special police were passing. I followed them toward Atocha, about a ten-minute walk, more and more fire trucks flashing by me, until I arrived at what they call a scene of mayhem. It was cloudy. There were police and medical workers and other people everywhere, many of them weeping and/or screaming, and, as I got closer to the station, more and more confusion. People streamed from the various exits, some of them wounded, lightly I guess, and emergency workers rushing in.

I saw, I might have seen, a dazed teenager with blood all over his face and a paramedic who took his arm and sat him down and gave him something that looked like an ice pack, instructing him to sit and hold it to his head. There was an odor of burnt plastic. Someone asked me what had happened. Helicopters beat the air overhead. I wandered around for a few minutes, found a wall to sit against, shut my eyes, and listened.

After I don't know how long, I stood and walked back toward and then up El Paseo del Prado, ambulances and people rushing past me. As I got farther away from the station I saw crowds in the doorways of bars and restaurants watching televisions and I could hear people saying "ETA" and quoting the estimated numbers of the dead, looking down toward the station and then back up at the screens. I reached the hotel lobby that was now packed and loud and took the elevator to my room; Isabel was gone. I felt in my pocket for my keys and rediscovered the necklace. I left the room, left the hotel, and walked up Huertas to my apartment. I climbed the stairs and took off my jacket and turned on my computer. It was almost ten. Surprised at how much time had passed, I opened a browser, called up the *New York Times,* and clicked on the giant headline. The article described the helicopters I could hear above me.

I wondered where Isabel had gone. Then I didn't. I made some coffee, took one white pill, climbed through the roof, and sat with the coffee and listened. After a while I dropped back down through the skylight, brushed my teeth again, and left my apartment. I went to the bank of pay phones in La Plaza Santa Ana and called Kansas with my calling card. For a while all the lines were in use and they could not complete my call. I kept trying and eventually got through. It was around four in the morning there. The phone rang its foreign ring and finally my mom picked up, still half-asleep. It's me, I said, and she asked what time is it, are you o.k. I said I was fine but there had been a terrorist attack. My dad was on the phone now, and asked me how far my apartment was from Atocha and I said I had been staying at the Ritz. This of course confused them both and again they asked if I was o.k. I hesitated and, voice cracking, said I had done a terrible thing. What, they said, and I told them that I had claimed in the presence of various people that my mom was dead or gravely ill and my dad was a fascist. Why, one of them asked, confused, but not upset. To get sympathy, I guessed. After a brief silence, my mom said she'd like to hear more about this later, but how many people had been killed, who was responsible, what was I going to do now, thank God I was o.k. I said I was exhausted and was going to try to sleep. They said that was a good idea and asked that I call them later, when it was night in Madrid. We said we loved each other and, before we hung up, my mom suggested I give blood.

I went back up to my apartment and refreshed the *Times;* the number of estimated dead was now around two hundred, at least a thousand injured. I considered walking back to Atocha, but instead I opened *El País* in another window and the *Guardian* in a third. I sat smoking and refreshing the home pages and watching the numbers change. I could feel the newspaper accounts modifying or replacing my memory of what I'd seen; was there a word for that feeling? The only other feeling I registered was fatigue. I fell asleep and when I awoke it was dark; I could hear café noise, albeit less than normal, in the plaza. I ate what there was to eat and read the news but my head was clouded; I could not process the conflicting theories regarding responsibility. The government maintained it was the separatists. I returned to La Plaza Santa Ana and called my parents again and my mom and I had a calmer version of the morning's conversation; I would explain the Ritz-Carlton thing later, I said. I returned to my apartment, undressed, and went back to sleep, this time in my bed, until late morning.

When I woke I read about the emerging link to Al Qaeda, although the government still claimed it was ETA, and I watched a terrible video online of Atocha's security camera footage, or was that many months later: an orange fireball bursting from a train, engulfing commuters with smoke, leaving the platform littered with bodies and stained with blood. There was to be a giant public demonstration against terrorism of all kinds that night across Spain. Even the king was going to march. I had lots of e-mails from friends and family and the foundation, none of which I read. I showered and left the apartment and walked toward Sol. There were trucks set up where you could give blood. I stood in line for a while at one of the trucks. When it was my turn, the woman asked me various questions about drugs, when I had eaten last, and other things I couldn't understand; I told her I felt sick and she impatiently waved me away and asked for the next person in line. I said to myself that, by that point, they didn't need blood for the injured anyway; they were probably still there only so people could feel like they were contributing; hadn't they done that in New York?

As I walked toward El Retiro I thought about how blood from my body might have been put into the body of someone injured by History. It was cloudy and cold. I didn't see anyone, not even the hash dealers. I sat for a while and then walked to the gallery, where Arturo and Rafa were. Later I learned that, while I was in the park, the entire city had emptied into the streets for a moment of silence without me. I was glad to see Arturo and Rafa and I told them so. We hugged each other and Arturo unloosed a torrent of language, saying he knew people who knew people who died, and speculating on what all this meant for the election, which was Sunday. If ETA were responsible, the Socialists, who were seen as weak on the separatists, would get destroyed. If it were Al Qaeda or other Islamic terrorists, the right-wing Aznar and his handpicked successor, Rajoy, were doomed; they had supported Bush's war, the fucking fascists. I asked them if ETA did it and they said they didn't believe it and something about tapes the police had found and it being the eleventh. While we were talking, Teresa arrived. She kissed me on both cheeks and scolded me for not having been around or writing her but she didn't seem angry. The conversation about the bombings and their political repercussions resumed and I was quiet. Then Arturo took a phone call and Rafa went to the back of the gallery for something, leaving Teresa and me alone. She said I looked tired and I said I had passed several long nights and she asked me, smiling, if I had passed them with this Isabel woman. Without emotion, I said I was never going to see Isabel again. Teresa squinted and said not to make any decisions on her account, but, smiling again, admitted she'd been a little jealous: very little. I waited to feel a thrill, however distant.

We went outside to smoke and I remembered the argument after my reading. I considered telling Teresa I had lied about my family but it no longer seemed significant. We decided to walk to a nearby restaurant for lunch. I tried to buy *El País* but the kiosks were out of them. "Collector items," Teresa said in English.

Neither of us ate much. We walked back to the gallery and I asked Arturo if they were still having the opening. He looked at me like I was crazy and said no. I must have looked ashamed, because he added, a little apologetically: but the paintings would still be on display and maybe people would gather in the gallery after the demonstration. I heard myself saying that he should cover one of the larger paintings with a black cloth as a memorial, a visual moment of silence. He thought this was a great idea and he started speaking at incomprehensible speed with Teresa; soon the decision was made that all the paintings would be covered for a couple of days, if they could get the painters to agree. Arturo started making calls again and Teresa asked me after a while if I wanted to look over my poems; I didn't. I told her I had written a lot of new stuff and pointed to the notebooks that were still on Arturo's desk. She opened the one on top and began to read with what looked like serious attention. Would they also cover the little placards bearing painters' names and prices?

Teresa read and read and I sat there blankly and every twenty minutes or so would go and smoke. Arturo had reached almost all of the painters and everyone had said yes; he had sent Rafa out for cloth. When Rafa returned he said the streets were filling for the demonstration and I could see from his hair that it had started raining. Teresa tore a corner of one of the pages of a book she had in her purse, a novel I think, and put it in my notebook to keep her place, which I knew I would, in retrospect, find touching. The gesture made me think of giving blood, but there was no real analogy. It looked like there was a crowd outside the gallery and I wondered if these were people Arturo knew who were waiting for us to join them, but when we exited the gallery, I realized this *was* the demonstration, that as far as I could see, the streets were full. A current of people, some with signs or candles, was moving slowly toward Colón, the central gathering point; from there the plan was to process toward Atocha. Many people weren't moving at all, as one was, wherever one was, already demonstrating. Teresa took my hand and I followed her into the current and we made our way to Colón, where the crowd was densest. Someone was speaking through a megaphone about peace and maybe about resilience. The rain intensified and umbrellas opened everywhere. I pictured how it must have looked from the helicopters. People were chanting that it wasn't raining, that Madrid was crying, and I thought this was a complicated chant, especially since it appeared to be spontaneous. Teresa and Arturo and Rafa were chanting, so I chanted too, but my voice sounded off to me, affected, and I worried it was conspicuous, that it failed to blend. I couldn't be the only one not chanting, so I mouthed the words. Eventually some portion of the crowd began to move in the direction of Atocha. We were walking slowly but it felt to me like we were standing still because so many people were moving in tandem. At one point I bent down, maybe to tie my shoe, and from my kneeling position I saw thousands of legs and I looked up a little and saw a more-or-less unbroken canopy formed by the umbrellas above me. Nearby some little kids were running around in this enclosed space formed by the bodies and umbrellas, maybe playing tag, hiding behind one pair of legs and then another. In retrospect, I would find this beautiful. When I stood up, Teresa was several feet away, other people between us. She was looking for but somehow didn't see me. I could have easily caught or called her, but I just stood there, letting the stream of bodies bend around me.

When she was gone I resumed moving toward Atocha. It must have been dark by then. I tried chanting, but quickly stopped. When we got to Huertas I turned away from the current and walked toward my apartment. Every street, even the little side streets branching off of Huertas, was packed with people. I eventually reached my apartment and pulled myself through the skylight and looked down at the sea of umbrellas, some of them softly illuminated, I guessed because they sheltered candles. I was looking away from Atocha but the crowd was continuous.

I realized at some point that I was freezing, dropped myself back through the skylight, and checked my e-mail. I answered friends and family, then read through the various e-mails from María José.

The first e-mails addressed to the group asked that all the fellows write her to confirm they were O.K. Then an e-mail addressed to the group said they had heard from all but one fellow. Then there was an e-mail just to me asking where I was. Two hundred people had been killed in a city of three million, I thought; what was the probability I had been among them? I went to *El País*'s home page and viewed the aerial photographs I had pictured in my mind. The crowds were audible in the apartment, but the noise was so constant it kept receding into the background. I opened the Tolstoy at random and started reading.

A few hours later I left my apartment. There were still people everywhere, but the demonstration was over. I walked, maybe through rain, back to the gallery; it was packed. There was a huge pile of umbrellas in the corner, an interesting sculpture. I thought some people recognized me, but I wasn't sure. The paintings were covered in what looked like black felt. I wondered if that would damage the paintings. The placards were uncovered. Toward the back of the gallery there was a bright light and I saw Arturo being interviewed by a reporter, presumably about the covered paintings. I was afraid that if he saw me he would credit me with the idea and would pull me in front of the camera, so I kept my distance. People were looking at the covered paintings as if they weren't covered, looking long and thoughtfully at the black felt and then reading the placard. I wondered if any of them would sell.

"I wonder if any of them will sell," Teresa said, suddenly beside me. Then she said, "Sorry we were separated." Maybe she'd seen me standing still, watching her get swept away. She had changed her clothes.

"Where do you live?" I asked her, apropos of nothing. I knew she had an apartment in Madrid but she had never invited me there and I had never asked to see it. She seemed to stay, at least half the time, at Rafa's.

She laughed at the question and said, "A fifteen-minute walk from here. You've walked me home before, remember?" I didn't.

"Can we go there?" I said. "I don't mean to fuck"—I couldn't think of any subtler Spanish word—"or anything. I am tired and the crowds—" I switched to English: "I'm just really out of it."

"I'll need to come back to help Arturo," she said in Spanish, "but we can go there for a while. You can stay there if you want. Arturo and Rafa will probably come back there later."

Teresa went to tell Arturo she was leaving and we emerged from the gallery into the rain and walked in silence until we reached Calle Serrano; I remembered her narrow, fancy building when we got there. She was on the top floor and we took the elevator, which had mirrored paneling. She had to turn her key in the elevator in order to get it to take us to her floor and when the elevator doors opened we were in her apartment. Besides the bathroom, the apartment was just one giant room with a very high ceiling and a balcony that overlooked Serrano. What furniture there was, was low to the ground: a desk in one corner, a red couch with a cat on it near the center of the room, and against one of the walls a low, Japanese-looking bed that was probably Swedish. There was a long coffee table near the couch. Piles of books were everywhere, but the piles somehow looked considered, tastefully arranged. The walls were empty save for various expensively framed and carefully grouped series of black-and-white photographs. I walked to the nearest bank of photographs. They showed very elegantly dressed men and women smoking and smiling. They looked like they were taken in the fifties. "Is this your family?" I asked Teresa, who was fixing drinks. "Distant family," she said. I wondered what it meant about your politics if you managed to be rich and fashionable in the Madrid of the fifties, but didn't ask.

I walked to another group of photographs and saw that they were Abel's idle machines, but much smaller than the photos in the gallery.

"You don't like them," she said, handing me a drink involving whiskey.

"They don't do much for me," I said in English. She squinted, maybe because of what I said, maybe because I'd once again used English.

"Make yourself at home," she said in English, as if quoting a movie, and I sat on the couch and the cat and I considered each other suspiciously. I asked if I could smoke, a silly question, and she indicated the ashtray and sat beside me and we both lit cigarettes. She walked with her cigarette and drink to a closet and somehow drank and smoked and changed her clothes in front of me without burning or spilling anything and without it seeming like a striptease.

"That's amazing," I said, vaguely.

She smiled as though she understood what I was referring to and sat back down beside me. I asked her if she knew anybody who died in the bombings. She said no. She said many of the dead were immigrants. She said that it was a crime against working people and that she didn't know many working people. Do you, she asked, and I thought for a while, then said I wasn't sure. She launched into a very detailed and, so far as I could tell, sophisticated projection of the political ramifications of the bombings. She was sure ETA had nothing to do with it. I didn't say anything. She went to a stereo I hadn't noticed and put on music.

The music filled the room and for a moment, maybe two measures, I felt intensely present. She said she should go back but that there was food and drink and clean towels. She had noticed I had smoked my last cigarette and pointed to a pack on the desk. She kissed me good-bye on the lips but it did not feel like an event.

When I was alone in the apartment I walked to her closet and looked through her clothes. I smelled one or two of the hanging dresses. There was a dresser inside the closet and I opened and shut the drawers. Then I went into the bathroom and looked around. Everything was spotless and I wondered if she cleaned it herself. Maybe an immigrant cleaned her apartment, an immigrant who'd been blown apart. There were a few bottles of pills behind the mirror but I couldn't tell what they were. Then I rolled a strong spliff with the last of the hash from my bag and smoked it on the balcony. When I was finished I took off my shoes and lay down on her bed. In the stack of books nearest her bed I saw a small poetry magazine from the u.s., an issue in which I was published. I was astonished that a tiny magazine published in New York featuring poems I had written in Providence about Topeka was here, in this gorgeous apartment in Madrid. Not that poems were *about* anything. Then I remembered I had given her the magazine. I removed it from the stack, knocking the stack over, and found my poem:

> Possessing a weapon has made me bashful.
> Tears appreciate in this economy of pleasure.
> The ether of data engulfs the capitol.
> Possessing a weapon has made me forgetful.
> My oboe tars her cenotaph.
> The surface is in process.
> Coruscant skinks emerge in force.
> The moon spits on a copse of spruce.
> Plausible opposites stir in the brush.
> Jupiter spins in its ruts.
> The wind extends its every courtesy.

I have never been here.
Understand?
You have never seen me.

———

I wasn't sure if Teresa had slept in the bed with me; there were sleeping bags and pillows on the floor, but they might have been Arturo's or Rafa's, neither of whom was in the apartment now. The sleeping bags made me think of body bags lined up beside the tracks, although I hadn't seen that yet. I had confused memories of people entering the apartment when I was half-asleep, snatches of their drunken conversation, the smell of marijuana, maybe a body next to me, breathing. Teresa was on the phone, speaking quietly so as not to wake me. I would not be able to ask her if she had slept in the bed; if she did, that would constitute a new level of intimacy and I could hardly admit I had no memory of it. For all I knew we'd kissed and fooled around; while I doubted that, I could imagine it in a way that felt like remembering.

The cat was still on the red couch, blinking. Although I had not made a noise or moved, Teresa knew I was awake, and brought me, phone tucked between ear and shoulder, an espresso; I hadn't heard the machine. I couldn't read her smile. I couldn't believe how good the coffee was. She went back to her desk and I sat up and finished the coffee and tried to listen to her conversation; she was saying something about making or receiving a delivery; maybe she did real work for the gallery. After my coffee I went into the bathroom and turned on the shower and shat and took one white pill and then stepped into the shower. The showerhead was elaborate and could be adjusted so as to texture the water in various ways. Somehow the showerhead, more than any other object in the apartment or the apartment itself, made me feel that Teresa's wealth was limitless. I realized I had not had water to drink, only coffee and alcohol, for what felt like an alarmingly long time. I opened my mouth and let it fill with water and swallowed.

I put on the same clothes and came out of the bathroom to find Teresa dressed, smoking and drinking her coffee on the red couch. She smiled at me, the cat blinked at me, and I said to her in English, "Everything here is beautiful. You are beautiful. The shower is beautiful. The coffee. How did you know I was awake? How was the beautiful coffee suddenly ready?" I sounded like I was translating from Spanish. "Why does everything in the apartment, from a pile of books to those papers on your desk, seem so beautifully arranged? How is it that your cat communicates so much intelligence, that it blinks so significantly?"

"Why are you speaking English?" she asked in English, widening her eyes.

"I don't know," I said in Spanish. Then I repeated in Spanish, to the best of my ability, everything I had just said about her, her dexterity, the shower, the coffee. She laughed at this but also looked a little sad. Then she said I must have really needed my sleep, that I'd slept deeply and for a long time. I wondered how she'd gauged its depth, if she'd tried to stir me. I did feel rested. The light in the apartment looked postmeridian.

"We should go to the protests," she said. I blinked at her and she explained: "There are protests at the PP headquarters. The PP was blaming ETA when it knew it wasn't responsible. People are furious," she said.

"Are you furious?" I asked.

"Arturo texted me," she said, ignoring my question. "He said there is a huge protest in front of the headquarters. A short walk from here." Then in English: "It's history in the making."

"If I hadn't woken up," I asked her with something strange in my voice, maybe anger, "would you have woken me or gone without me or just not gone?"

"I don't know," she said. "You woke up." Her eyes were wide again.

We left the apartment, walked a few blocks, and before we saw the crowd, we heard it, chanting about truth and lies and fascism. Police in riot gear stood between the crowd and PP headquarters. The crowd was young and angry and we joined them. Teresa, to my surprise, blended in gracefully, taking up the chant, although I couldn't pick out her voice particularly, and pumping her fist in the air with the rest of the crowd without any of it seeming affected or silly. People were banging on drums and pots and pans and I followed Teresa deeper into the crowd. Finally I could go no farther and she disappeared in front of me. I felt she knew she'd lost me, and wondered if she was responding to my standing still at the protests the previous day. A police officer said something on a megaphone and the chants intensified. I thought the building might be stormed, but it wasn't. I slipped back out of the crowd and crossed the street and watched the protest from there. For a second I thought I saw Isabel.

After I don't know how long, Teresa emerged from the crowd and found me. She was with a man I didn't recognize. Even from far away, I could tell that he was handsome. When they reached me she spoke to me in English.

"Where did you go?" she said. And when I didn't respond, she said in Spanish, "This is Carlos."

I shook Carlos's hand as jealousy spread through my body. He was a full six inches taller than I was.

We stood together and faced the protest. The crowd had expanded so that now, while we were still apart from it, we were close enough that our presence expressed fellowship. Without warning and with improbable volume, Carlos started a chant about Rajoy. He was bellowing, and yet he seemed completely calm. At first he was the only one chanting his chant and I hoped nobody would pick it up, that he would have to abandon it, embarrassed. But then the other people who were near the crowd but not part of it joined Carlos in chanting. And once the people who were near the crowd were linked by the chant, they moved and we moved with them into the crowd and were absorbed. Then Carlos's chant spread from our part of the crowd forward and grew deafening. Carlos's voice was no longer distinct and I looked at his handsome face and hated it.

Again I retreated and Teresa saw me go and just waved good-bye and I felt annihilated. I tried to smile at her in a manner that doubted her politics, doubted her place in the crowd, but could not. I wound my way through various small streets until I found myself near Sol. From there I walked to my apartment and once in my apartment read about the unfolding events of which I'd failed to form a part. The elections were tomorrow. I tried to think about whether public outrage would cost the PP the elections, about blood on the platform and the makeshift morgue in the convention center near Atocha, but instead I imagined making love with Teresa as if I were remembering it. Then I imagined her fucking Carlos and felt sure that when I left they had gone immediately back to her apartment. I tried to think about Isabel, could not, but was reminded of the necklace, which I took out of its case. It felt like I'd been carrying it for years. I put it back in its case and left the apartment for the jewelers to see if I could return it. By the time I reached the jewelers I doubted I would have the courage to face the woman who sold it to me; I was relieved to find the store was closed.

I walked to the Reina Sofía, bought a ticket, and wandered through the giant Calder exhibit. The museum was almost empty.

The large white rooms reminded me of Teresa's apartment and I imagined sleeping with both Carlos and Teresa at the same time and being humiliated by his beauty and size. I pictured giving Teresa the necklace, how she would accept it graciously but without surprise or emotion and I was furious at her. There was a very young museum guard, a teenager, sending a text beneath a giant mobile. I approached her and said that I had bought a necklace for my girl-friend but that we had broken up and I was leaving the country the next day; I didn't want the necklace, would she like it. Without giving her time to answer, I handed her the case and walked away.

From the museum I went to the café where I took my lunch almost daily and ordered one of the hard sandwiches and a watery beer. When I had finished my meal I was surprised that it was dusk, I must have slept very late, and I walked into El Retiro to buy more hash. I scoured the park but could not find a dealer anywhere. It occurred to me that they'd probably been rounded up by the police, questioned, and perhaps deported since, as I had read, there was some speculation that the bombers had come from North Africa. I sat on a bench and watched the wind in the old-world trees and said to myself that I would not go to Teresa's apartment or the gallery. I swore that I would wait for her to come to me and if she never came, so be it. But then I said to myself that History was being made and that I needed to be with Spaniards to experience it; I should at least try to find Arturo. I knew I was only elaborating an excuse to see Teresa. I tried to justify my pettiness by meditating on the relation of the personal to the historical but my meditations did not go far; I stood, absently checked my pockets for tranquilizers, and began to walk quickly through the thickening dusk.

I was lost for a little while but eventually found her building, rang the bell, and was immediately buzzed in. As the elevator slowly ascended—it worked without the key—I began to hear music and voices and laughter; I was still attempting to compose my face when the doors opened. There were a lot of people, Teresa and Rafa the only two I knew, smoking and drinking and talking animatedly about the protests and elections. Several people were on phones. I looked around for Carlos but did not see him and a wave of relief broke over me. Teresa was on the red sofa admiring another woman's earrings; she did not stand to greet me. I walked to Rafa, who was looking through Teresa's music, and asked him where Arturo was as if it were important that I find him. Without listening to his response I walked out onto the balcony and lit a cigarette and there was Carlos, smoking with two other men. Carlos smiled a smile I experienced as triumphant, postcoital, and said hello. He did not introduce me to his friends, who struck me as stylish and hostile; they were heavily and expensively tattooed. I grinned at the friends in a way that suggested I would slit their throats if given the chance and echoed Carlos's greeting. I wasn't sure what to do; I could not return to the apartment without it seeming like a retreat and I was too full of jealousy to attempt casual speech. Finally Carlos said something to me about how this must be an interesting time to be an American in Spain. I said it was, ignoring the derision with which he'd pronounced "American." What did I think, he said. About what, I asked. About everything, he said. I looked off in the distance as though I was making an effort to formulate my complex reaction so simply even an idiot like him might understand. Then, as if concluding this was an impossible task, I said I didn't know.

"I enjoyed your poetry reading a few months ago," said one of his friends. He sounded gentle and sincere and I was bewildered. I wondered if Carlos in fact was being completely friendly, if I was only projecting my jealousy. I felt a little crazy and remembered puking in the bathroom at Zalacaín.

"Thanks," I said.

"Are you going to write a poem about the bombings?" Carlos asked, the mockery unmistakable. I wanted to throw him from the balcony. I finished my cigarette before saying no.

I walked back into the apartment, saw a space beside Teresa on the couch, and sat down. She started playing with my hair and I said to her in English that Carlos might get jealous; she ignored me. I wanted to kiss her but didn't. I took a book from a stack nearby and feigned interest, thrilled she was flirting with me in plain sight. After a while Carlos and his friends returned and Carlos said something to a few of the other people milling around and then said to Teresa that they were going to rejoin the protest, that he would text her later. O.K., she said, smiling at him the same way she had smiled at me. They kissed each other on both cheeks and while he was near her ear he whispered something and she laughed. "Later," he said to me, and I said good-bye as if I couldn't quite remember who he was.

Soon the other guests, including Rafa, left the apartment, presumably for the protest. I continued to look at the book, a novel by Cela. Teresa went to her desk and when she came back she had a thin joint, which she lit and passed to me. It was weed, not hash. When we finished she went to her closet and began to change. I rose and walked to her and held her from behind and kissed her on the neck. She turned to me and we kissed for a while but for reasons mysterious to me, that was that. I sat back down and she finished changing and then sat beside me and resumed doing the thing with my hair and asked if I wanted to find the protests. I said I was too high and she squinted and said she felt she needed to go. I didn't say anything. She said I could stay there and read or whatever until she returned. I thought of Carlos.

"What did that guy say to you when he left?" I asked.

"What guy?" she asked.

"Carlos," I said.

"Nothing," she said.

"He whispered something to you when he was saying good-bye and you laughed," I reminded her.

"I don't remember," she lied. I was furious.

"When do you think you'll be back?" I asked, careful not to reveal my anger.

"I'm not sure," she said.

"If it's o.k., I will stay here for a while. Then I have to meet someone," I said.

"o.k.," she said. I couldn't believe she wasn't going to ask me who. "Take those keys," she said, pointing to a hook by the door. "You can leave the elevator unlocked; the bigger key is for the front," she said.

"o.k.," I said, my fury tempered by the offer of the keys.

"Let's go over the poems tomorrow," she said. "I want to select a couple of the new ones to translate."

"Sure," I said. I didn't care about the poems.

"Unless you don't care about the poems," she said. Her eyes were neither wide nor squinted and she was not smiling. I was pleased to see her angry.

"I'm not very interested in poetry at a time like this," I said, suggesting she was focused on petty personal concerns at a moment of historical unrest. "Tomorrow is the election," I said, as though she might have forgotten.

She looked angrier. "And what are you planning to do tomorrow?" she asked. "How are you going to participate in this historic moment?"

"It's not my country," I said, my face asserting this statement had many simultaneous registers of significance. I thought I saw her sound them in her head.

"Bueno," she said, which can mean anything, and left.

I walked onto the balcony to find it was fully night and watched her go. When I couldn't see her anymore I went back into the apartment. I looked around her desk, found what looked like a diary, and opened it; it was full of poems in what I supposed was her hand. They were replete with words I didn't know and that I assumed must be very specific nouns: grackle, night-blooming jasmine, hollow-point shells—I had no idea. I assigned a meaning more or less at random to each unfamiliar word and then the poems were lovely. I began to read one aloud but my voice sounded strange in the empty apartment and I stopped, again remembering Zalacaín. I searched the journal to see if there were peoples' names in any of the poems, Adán, Carlos, etc.; there weren't. On one of the pages there was a stain, probably coffee, but it made me think of blood. I imagined Teresa writing in the journal on a train and I imagined the train exploding.

I put the journal down. I felt stupid for not going to the protests and decided I would find them, find Teresa. I took the keys and left, walking first to PP headquarters. Nobody was there except a few journalists, a few police. I asked a teenager on a bench where the protests were; he just laughed at me. I walked to Colón but the plaza was empty. From Colón I moved up El Paseo de Recoletos, which became El Paseo del Prado. It felt strange to be looking for a crowd, to be wandering around in search of History or Teresa. I walked all the way to Atocha. I saw candles and small groups of people but no protest. For the first time since I had been in Spain, I wished I had a phone. I walked back down El Paseo del Prado and onto Huertas. I passed a bar that had a TV on and I could see images of a swarming crowd. I went in and ordered a whiskey and saw the protestors in front of the PP headquarters. At first I thought it was footage from earlier in the day, but then I noticed it was dark. Is this living, I asked the bartender, pointing to the screen. He blinked at me. Is this live, I corrected myself. He nodded. I drank and watched and eventually went home and fell sleep.

———

While Spain was voting I was checking e-mail. According to the internet, protests continued at the PP headquarters. Then, while Spain was voting, someone rang my buzzer. I thought it was Teresa and I was about to let her in when I realized it might be Isabel, whom I did not want to see. I decided to risk it, hit the buzzer, and heard someone running up the steps. By the time I heard a knock at my door I had deduced it was Arturo; he was the only person I knew who would run. I opened the door and he looked excited, like he hadn't had much sleep. He sat down and asked for a cigarette and I gave him one and he lit it and began to speak. He said those fascist bastards were going to lose and Zapatero would win and while Zapatero wasn't a radical, he was O.K. He said they had been up all night protesting and partying. I asked if those were the same thing, protesting and partying. He smiled inscrutably and I wondered where they had learned to smile that way, then thought I remembered that smile on the faces of the elegant people in the old photographs in Teresa's apartment.

"Did you vote?" I asked him.

"I don't vote," he said.

"Why?" I asked.

"I don't believe in it," he said.

"Why?" I asked.

"I won't participate in a corrupt system," he said. He said it like he'd said it many times that day.

"Does Teresa vote?" I wondered.

"Yes," he said, but it sounded like he wasn't sure.

"And Carlos?" I asked, as if I knew all about Carlos.

"Carlos is a Marxist," Arturo said, picking up one of the volumes of Tolstoy and flipping through it.

"A Marxist," I repeated. "How long have you known Carlos?" It occurred to me that I didn't know if there was an active Communist party in Spain.

"Forever," he said, still looking at the book. "But Carlos votes."

I don't know why I was surprised: "Really?"

"Yes, but he votes for the wrong side on purpose," he explained.

"He votes for the PP," I exclaimed in disbelief.

"He votes to exacerbate the system's contradictions," is what I guessed Arturo said.

"That fucker," I said in English. Arturo looked up at me. "He votes to make things worse," I confirmed in Spanish.

"Yes," he said, and repeated the thing about contradictions as though he'd said it many times that day. "Carlos wants a revolution."

"What kind of revolution?" I asked, making no effort to contain my disdain.

"Don't worry about Carlos," he said, smiling again. "Teresa doesn't love him."

"I'm not worried," I lied. "He should vote for the Socialists," I said.

"Carlos doesn't believe in socialism," Arturo said. "If the Socialists win, we're having a big party at Rafa's. If the PP wins, there will be more protests. Maybe riots. Teresa wanted me to tell you, and to say that you should come with us."

I thought about saying I was busy, but said, "O.K."

"We'll pick you up at nine either way," he said. And, as he stood to leave, "If you're going to stay in Spain, you should get a phone." I wondered what he meant by "stay."

The Socialists won. The American media were furious, claiming the Spanish had been intimidated by terrorism. Outside I heard people cheering. A little before ten the buzzer rang and I went downstairs and Teresa was there. She kissed me on the lips and I felt in love with her. We walked together to the car, where Arturo was waiting. It took us a long time to get beyond the city. Arturo talked to Teresa the whole drive, something about how Pedro Almodóvar had said on TV that the PP was planning a coup, but I might have misunderstood. When we finally arrived at Rafa's expansive house I asked how Rafa made his money. They laughed. I said I meant how did his family make its money. Teresa said something about banks. And your own family, I asked, tentatively. Arturo said they didn't make it by writing poetry and we laughed. Then Teresa said she had told me already, didn't I remember. I hesitated and said yes, I remember now. She might have told me the first night I met her. Or she might have told me at various points and I failed to understand her Spanish. Or she might have been lying about having told me. We went inside.

Beautiful people were there again, a few of whom I recognized from the gallery or Teresa's apartment. Everything was a little changed, a little charged. For whatever reason I thought again of the photographs of Teresa's distant family. I didn't know how to compose my face, if indifference tinged with vague disdain was still the right expression. If I could have smiled Teresa's inscrutable smile, I would have. One of the paintings was covered with black felt. It didn't look like a covered painting from the nineteenth century; it looked like contemporary art. People were talking about politics, or everything seemed suddenly political. I overheard conversations about the role of photography *now,* where "now" meant post–March 11. A "post" was being formed, and the air was alive less with the excitement of a period than with the excitement of periodization. I heard something about how the cell phone, instrumental to organizing the marches, was the dominant political technology of the age. What about Titadine, the form of compressed dynamite used in the attacks, I wanted to say; wasn't that the dominant technology? I said this to Teresa, who corrected me gently as we poured ourselves drinks: these attacks were "made for tv"; she said the phrase in English.

I meant to pour myself gin, but when I tried it, I discovered it was silver tequila. At seventeen I had made myself violently ill drinking tequila and had never had it again, except to taste it every couple of years to see if it still disgusted me, which it always did. I thought back to that night in Topeka, vomiting for an hour near a bonfire and then sleeping in the bed of a pickup in the middle of the winter. I could smell the campfire and felt cold and a little dizzy. Then I thought of Cyrus trying to wash the taste out of his mouth. Teresa took the drink from me and handed me a fresh one, a vodka tonic, which smelled clean. You don't want tequila, she said, as though she knew what I was remembering, as though we had known each other for many years. I was becoming almost frightened of her grace and gifts of anticipation; I worried that I would not be able to lie to her, and I worried, not for the first time, that whenever I'd thought I'd successfully lied to her, she had in fact easily seen through me. If I were forced to rely on only the literal truth, she would soon grow tired of me. I thought I would attempt to preempt or slow this situation by naming it, and as we walked out back with our drinks, I said to her in English, "You are the most graceful and protean person I know. The way you handed me the coffee right when I awoke or the way just now you took the tequila from me or," I paused to think of an example not involving drinks, "the way you can move without apparent transition from your stylish apartment to a protest."

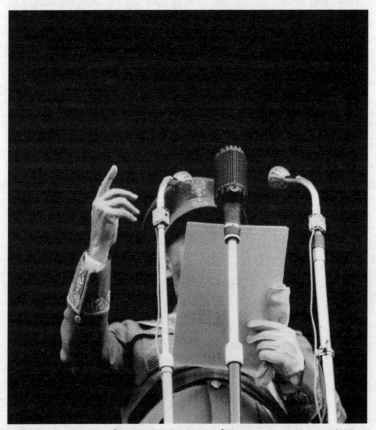

"The proper names of leaders are distractions from concrete economic modes."

"Why do you keep speaking to me in English?" she asked, with something like concern.

I ignored the question and went on, "But I'm worried you're too cool for me, that you'll realize I'm in fact a fraud. An inelegant fraud. I won't be able to fool you and you'll get bored." As I said this, I thought it would be impossible to hide my pills from her. I had a sudden, involuntary memory of the Ritz.

"All you're describing," she said in Spanish, "is the personality of a translator. From apartment to protest, from English to Spanish." If she had spoken in English, I would have found it a little grand; in Spanish I experienced it as profound. I wondered if she'd weighed the sentence in both languages before selecting the one that would produce the desired effect.

Teresa started to remove her clothes and for a second I thought she had lost her mind. But she had a swimsuit on underneath, and she left her clothes in a little pile and slipped noiselessly into the heated, lighted pool, as if to punctuate the ease with which she could move between media. There were a few other people in the pool, all of them women, all of whom appeared to know Teresa. I found a nearby patio chair and lit a cigarette, reiterating to myself my promise that I would never smoke another cigarette once I left Madrid, but that until then I gave myself permission to smoke without guilt. This little psychological mechanism, as crucial to my smoking as lighter or match, reminded me of Arturo's comment about staying in Spain. I saw Teresa dive underwater and thought, why wouldn't I stay? I could make enough money teaching English to keep the same apartment. Maybe Arturo would pay me to work at the gallery in some capacity. Maybe my parents would send me money. Or maybe Teresa would support me. I would write and she would translate and we would walk through El Retiro at dusk. I imagined people visiting from the U.S., imagined their amazement and envy at the life I had made for myself. How long would I stay beyond the fellowship, I wondered. Maybe another year; I would make myself really learn Spanish, which seemed dimly possible now, and I would also begin to translate

Teresa's poems into English. I would publish a book of poems and then a book of translations and I would come home, perhaps with Teresa, as a celebrated author imbued with Iberian mystery. Or would I never go home, except to visit? I finished my drink and went to the bar for another and there was the man who had argued with Abel after my reading, the man who believed the disjunction of my poetry was a radical political gesture.

He recognized me, but he misremembered our conversation. "Do you still believe that poetry can change the world?" he asked me.

I paused. "It can exacerbate the world's contradictions," I said, mumbling the verb I didn't really know.

"Well, it's not poetry that makes things happen," he said.

"Poetry makes nothing happen," I said in English. He blinked at me. "What made all of this," I said in Spanish, waving my hand to include the party in the events of the last few days, "happen?"

"Bodies in the streets," he said. At first I thought he meant dead bodies; then I realized he meant the bodies of protestors. I tried to describe that confusion, the two ways one could understand his answer, but I garbled the Spanish and abandoned the thought.

I went back outside and sat in the same chair and drank my drink. Teresa was no longer in the pool and I looked around for her but couldn't see her. When my drink was finished I fixed another, this time at the little outside bar, and then I walked beyond the pool toward the softly lit garden where I had once heard Rafa sing. When I encountered Teresa sitting on the stone bench kissing Carlos, my jealousy and rage felt like solid things, things formed over many years, so it seemed like they preceded their cause, were detached from the scene. It was a while before I noticed two of the other swimmers nearby, maybe five feet from the bench, faint glow of white towels, sharing a joint. I sat down beside them and one of them passed me the joint, saying something like, "Here is the poet." Teresa had stopped kissing or letting herself be kissed by the man who I now saw was not Carlos, was another handsome man I didn't know; she had noticed me, entirely without concern. I considered getting up and storming off to the edge of the property overlooking the hill where I had told Teresa my mother was dead. I imagined striking the man, who was walking back to the party now, repeatedly in the face. The joint was before me again and the woman who passed it began to speak to me and either because I was high or upset I couldn't understand her Spanish, but that's not really right. Her Spanish, like Teresa's poem, became a repository for whatever meaning I assigned it, and I felt I understood, although I knew I was talking to myself. It was as if she said: Think about the necklace. Think about the making of the necklace. About Isabel's brother's notebook. I could hear what she was actually saying beneath this and I heard myself respond but all of that was very distant. It was as if she said: Imagine her brother writing. Think of the little scrap of paper Teresa tore from her novel and put into your notebook. Think of the hash transported inside one body as a solid and expelled and sold and then drawn into your body as vapor and gas. Think of the bombers purchasing the backpacks. Always think of the objects. Think of the necklaces and novels and bodies torn apart by the blast. Think of the making of the necklaces and the novels and the bodies and Isabel's brother in the crushed red car. But then think of a poster of Michael Jordan on the wall of Isabel's brother's room while he wrote the years down in the notebook. Where is that poster now. And think of the field opposite the telephone pole her brother wrapped the car around. How you can turn your attention away from the crushed red car and his body and walk into the field where nothing is happening, just indifferent wind in the indifferent grass, but a particular wind in particular grass. You can stay there for as long as you want, easily blocking out the sirens. Or you can enter the poster with the sea of camera flashes as Michael Jordan jumps and you can leave the arena as the crowd is roaring and walk into the Chicago of the recent past where novels are being written and necklaces are being made and gases are being inhaled and dates are being memorized by brains and brains destroyed in crashes. You can see all of this from a great height and zoom out until it is no longer visible or you can zoom in on the writing hand or the face of the dead, zoom in until it's no longer a face. Or you can click on something and drag it. You can adjust the color or you can make it black and white. You can view any object from any angle or multiple angles simultaneously or you can shut your eyes and listen to the crowd in the arena or the sirens slowly approaching the red car or the sound of the pen writing down the years as silver is hammered and shaped.

Teresa had sat down beside us and lit another joint and passed it to me and asked me something and I heard myself respond but all that was very distant and what I heard her whispering was something like: To join lips to express affection or as part of insufflation. To click the teeth while making love or trying to form a seal between your mouth and the victim's or to place the tongue between your teeth to pronounce the z of Zalacaín or to place a tooth beneath a pillow or the bracelet made of baby teeth her grandma had. To attempt to move from one language into another without rotation or angular displacement and to fail in that attempt and call your father from a pay phone weeping or to weep before a painting so one can think of pay phones and of paintings as the same. Now I realized Teresa wasn't speaking but was humming and playing with my hair but still I heard: To embrace the tragic interchangeability of nouns and smile inscrutably or to find a way of touching down, albeit momentarily, and be made visible by swirling condensation and debris and to know that one pole of experience is always caught up in the other but to know this finally in your body, cone of heat unfurling. To take everything personally until your personality dissolves and you can move without transition from apartment to protest or distribute yourself among a shifting configuration of bodies, saying yes to everything, affirming nothing, your own body "giving up / Its shape in a gesture that expresses that shape."

Then I was on my back and Teresa was on her back beside me and all of the jealousy was gone or so far away I no longer thought of it as mine. I could see a particularly bright star that I then saw as a satellite but ultimately I knew it was a plane.

5

I WAS IN NO POSITION TO EVALUATE HER TRANSLATIONS BUT I SENSED they were very good. When she read them to me I felt that she had carried a delicate, mirrored thing down a treacherous path, but what that thing was, I had no idea, and "path" isn't really the word. Arturo had ceded the project entirely to Teresa. We had culled fifteen pages or so of what we thought were the better poems. I was flattered and mystified and made a little uneasy by Teresa's apparently intense and sincere enthusiasm for my writing. Often when I slept at her place she would, instead of coming to bed with me, go to her desk and work, presumably on my poems. We never fucked or made love or had sex; I wasn't sure why, but I associated that fact with the translations. And when she was smiling her inscrutable smile or attending to me with her uncanny grace, producing the match or coffee or phrase I wanted before I knew I wanted it, or when we were just walking around Madrid in silence, I felt she was observing me, observing me with interested detachment, ridiculous phrase, as if my behavior might hold clues for her regarding a resonance or inflection or principle of lineation. She never mentioned her own poetry.

In post–March 11 Madrid, I kept thinking things were going to explode; I would watch the planes making their way to Barajas and the sun would catch them briefly and I would believe for a second, with less fear than excitement, that they were aflame. Or I would take the Metro and experience a sudden jerk in the carriage as the first detonation. I would imagine my friends from the U.S., their amazement and maybe envy at the death I had made for myself, how I'd been contacted by History. Why I thought, why everybody thought, that dying in a terrorist attack was more bound up with the inexorable logic of History than dying in a car crash or from lung cancer, I couldn't really say. I told Teresa that it derived from our impoverished sense of the political, that we could not think of the car or cigarette as Titadine because that would force us to confront our economic mode; when she said I sounded like Carlos, my face burned. Where is Carlos anyway, I asked her one afternoon as we walked slowly toward her apartment from La Filmoteca. We had seen two movies by Cocteau, the subject of a retrospective. It was one of the first hot days and the entire city, save Teresa, appeared sluggish. She said Carlos was in Barcelona, working. In my mind Carlos and Oscar, near anagrams, merged, and I had a sudden pang of longing for Isabel. I asked her what kind of work he did and she said, in English for some reason, "Organizing."

"I have never been to Barcelona," I said. The notion of Carlos "organizing," I hoped she understood, was too preposterous to acknowledge.

"We can get there in a few hours on AVE," she said, which was the high-speed train. I had thought it took much longer.

"Why, do you want to see Carlos?" I asked.

"We can go back to my apartment and get some clothes and go tonight, if you want," she ignored me.

"O.K.," I said, and we walked more quickly to the apartment, packed a few things, including, I saw, the notebooks of my poems and her translations, and then took a cab to Atocha to catch the next train. She bought the tickets because she bought everything and we walked past some red candles and boarded the train and after an initial jerk that I thought was an explosion we were speeding north, images from Cocteau's *Orpheus* still flashing in my head. Three hours later we were in Barcelona. We walked from the station into El Barrio Gótico, labyrinthine, medieval streets largely closed to cars, and arrived at what looked like a fancy private residence but was in fact a small hotel. Teresa greeted a woman behind the tall desk and said something, to my surprise, in fluent Catalan. She gave her a credit card and we were provided an antiquated key. We ascended two flights of iron stairs and found our room. It had a giant wooden door, high ceilings, and the walls were white, so it recalled Teresa's apartment. Teresa removed more clothes from her small bag than I would have thought possible and hung them in the closet. Why weren't they wrinkled? We walked onto the balcony overlooking the street; it was only now dark.

She asked me what I would like to do and I said I was hungry; there was a restaurant she liked near the Sagrada Familia. We left the hotel, walked for a while, and emerged onto Las Ramblas. We took a cab to the Sagrada Familia, which was illuminated; it was the ugliest building I had ever seen. A few blocks away was the restaurant, Alkimia, full of fashionable people, and although it was crowded and we had no reservation we were immediately seated. I ordered a drink in Spanish and the waiter clarified my order in English, something that never happened in Madrid. Teresa ordered various small plates and they came quickly: tuna belly cut in the manner of Iberian ham and served over some kind of broad bean; white bread rubbed in oil and covered with tomato paste; a dish involving truffles and tiny pieces of sausage that might have been duck; it was all delicious. They brought us a bottle of white wine I hadn't heard Teresa order and by dessert I felt pleasantly drunk. Dessert was a wonderful and unfamiliar ice cream and I asked the waiter what was in it and he said "Eucalyptus." I was slow to recognize the gorgeous word as English.

After dinner we sat on a bench in a little park full of people and beneath a branching cast-iron street lamp a small wave of euphoria broke over me. Teresa let herself be kissed for a while and then we took a cab back to the outskirts of El Barrio Gótico and walked to our hotel and I thought we might make love. Instead we smoked another spliff on the balcony and I asked her how she learned Catalan. She said she had lived in Barcelona at various points, said it as if she were very old; Arturo had told me she was twenty-seven; she looked older and younger than her age in shifts. I said I would like to have a drink and we left again and after ten minutes or so we descended a few stairs into a bar that felt like a cave, cool and dark. We seated ourselves in green leather chairs in a corner around a little table that seemed to be made of petrified wood. A woman with an array of facial piercings appeared at our table and we ordered our drinks. Teresa asked me if I had seen the Antonioni movie partially set in Barcelona, *The Passenger*, and, lying, I said of course. She said I had his eyebrows, Jack Nicholson, that I called on my eyebrows to do important work, that if she were deaf she would read my eyebrows, not my lips. I said she was simply describing the personality of the translator, but I said it in my head. She said Arturo always claimed she looked like Maria Schneider, whom I knew from *Last Tango in Paris*, which I hated, and I could see what Arturo meant. I wondered what Maria Schneider's relationship to Jack Nicholson was in *The Passenger*, what kind of statement Teresa was making about our relationship, and based on the Antonioni films I knew, I guessed it was unflattering.

"How do you understand their relationship?" I asked, trying to sound as though I'd pondered it for years.

"I don't understand it," she said, making it clear that was the point. Then she said things I could barely follow about the penultimate shot in the film, a continuous shot taken at "magic hour," a phrase she said in English. I couldn't understand what the shot looked like, but I understood that Antonioni had built, in order to achieve it, a special camera enclosed in a plastic sphere and fitted with various gyroscopes, whatever those were.

We ordered fresh drinks and Teresa talked about films, almost none of which I knew; maybe because we'd seen *Orpheus,* a movie about fluid boundaries, earlier that day, or because we were suddenly and impulsively arrived in a new city, or maybe because the bar was like a cave, I projected images to accompany her speech. Teresa appeared in those images, entered the films she was describing, and soon the films collapsed into one film, and it was her life I was imagining. She didn't so much recount plots as shots and sequences as though they were plots. I pictured her at various ages and at the center of each scene, as if she had organized it around herself, and this struck me as a higher form of biography than the mere detailing of events. The more she talked the less aware of my presence she seemed; after several rounds, she asked for the check without consulting me and paid.

We left the bar and wound through the narrow streets and soon were back at our hotel. I rolled a spliff and asked her if she wanted any and she said no and I lay in bed smoking while she sat at the little table in the corner and worked on the translations, opening my notebook and hers. I asked her if she wanted to read me some and she again said no. I didn't understand her method. She had no dictionary and asked no questions and I wondered if she was translating at all. After a while she came to bed and shut her eyes and I tried in my clumsy way to initiate some contact but she was totally if somehow gently unresponsive and soon she was asleep. For a long time, I watched her breathe.

When I woke she was reading Ashbery beside me. I wondered if she'd seen the pills in my bag. She smiled to indicate whatever distance had established itself between us the previous night had closed. Her breath smelled terrible and I told myself to commit that fact to memory, to remember it the next time I was intimidated by her unwavering grace. I told her I was going out for coffee. I got dressed, took my bag, and stumbled downstairs and out onto the street and walked until I found a café. Right as I was about to order, I realized I had no money; I left the café to find an ATM. Eventually the stone street widened into a modern avenue and I found a Deutsche Bank, where I withdrew the unreal currency. Still half-asleep, I put the cash in my wallet, and began to walk in what I thought was the direction I had come from, but after a few blocks I realized I was wrong. I retraced my steps and passed the bank but my confusion deepened; maybe I'd been right before. I asked a man, probably Roma, who was sitting in a doorway, where El Barrio Gótico was. He pointed and, although I headed in that direction for many minutes, I couldn't find the ancient streets. I decided to have some coffee and entered the next café and ordered an espresso, asking the man who served me for directions. He drew me a confusing map on a napkin and I thanked him, deciding to take a cab.

Then I saw Isabel pass by. I had often thought I'd seen Isabel over the last month or two. This time I felt sure, despite the improbability, and I put down various large coins without finishing my coffee and set off after her. It wasn't until I was in pursuit that I wondered why I wanted to catch her; I had nothing to say, though I had the indeterminate sense I owed her an apology. She crossed a busy street and by the time I got there the traffic was flowing and I had to wait. It took forever for the light to change and I wasn't sure it was still her I was trailing but I pursued a woman with something in her hair; she ultimately disappeared around a curve. I stopped again and asked a woman selling cut flowers how to get to El Barrio Gótico and she gave me Metro directions. I thanked her and flagged a cab. When we arrived at the neighborhood's edge, I went again in search of coffee. I found a café, bought two espressos to go, and walked deeper into the neighborhood, turning onto a street I thought I recognized. I did not know the name of the hotel. Soon I noticed the coffee was cold and I drank mine quickly and threw both cups away. I felt irritated and stupid and sat down on a bench to let my head clear. A blind man was selling lottery tickets nearby, shouting something about fate. I felt like a character in *The Passenger,* a movie I had never seen.

When I resumed my search I gradually realized I no longer remembered what the façade of the nameless hotel looked like exactly; I could have passed it many times already. I didn't have Teresa's phone number. I estimated an hour and a half had elapsed since I left. Hungry, I entered yet another café and ordered yet another coffee and also a piece of tortilla, which I hated before it arrived. I told the waiter I was looking for a hotel whose name I didn't know on a street whose name I didn't know and could he help me; we both laughed and he said: Aren't we all. When I finished eating I tried again, feeling like an actor whose wanderings were being used as an excuse to shoot the scenery. After I don't know how long, surely more than an hour, I found myself in a small plaza and sat down, defeated. My irritation turned to worry; it simply would not be believable to me if I were Teresa that I had left the hotel to get us coffee and had gotten lost for however many hours would have passed by the time I found her. And even if it were somehow believable, I didn't like what such a story would do to her image of me, an image about which I was actively, maybe increasingly, concerned. I would fare better in her eyes, I thought, to disappear mysteriously for several days than to show up like a lost child, dirty and exhausted, as night fell. With something like desperation, I resumed my wanderings. I started to feel a little crazy, space curling around the edges, which reminded me to take my white pill. I found another bench and sat down, stomping to scatter the pigeons. Without texture, time passed.

I arose and walked until I emerged onto Las Ramblas, where there were crowds around various men who were covered in body paint and pretending to be statues. They moved suddenly, scaring the children, when you gave them coins. I continued down Las Ramblas and onto the pier. There was a small outdoor bar on the little stretch of beach and I sat under the red plastic awning and ordered patatas bravas and a beer. I drank the beer quickly and ordered another. A funicular descended from the hills to a point near the beach. There were many teenagers in bathing suits although the water must have been cold. A small wave of sexual desire broke over me. When I finished the second beer I walked back to Las Ramblas, drifted for a while, then flagged down a cab and went to the Picasso Museum. Teresa had mentioned wanting to show it to me; maybe she would be there.

I stood, I made myself stand, in front of the early portrait of his mother. It yielded nothing. The woman, in profile, is half-asleep; her head is leaning slightly forward and her eyes are closed. Pastel on paper. 1896. He was what, fifteen? A freak of nature. I could convince myself I saw space curling around the figure or areas where space flattened suddenly, but I did not see this. Maybe I did see, however, the self-assurance of a painter who assumed his juvenilia would one day be scoured for the seeds of genius, embarrassing phrase. If the work felt uncanny, it was because it was mortgaged; it was borrowing from future accomplishment as much as pointing to it. It had started to rain a little; I could hear it falling on the skylight.

I wondered how my project would have differed if I'd come to Barcelona instead of Madrid. I thought of this in order to avoid thinking about Teresa, wherever she was. That I was contingent, interchangeable, I took as a given. Slightly more impetuous brush-strokes in the self-portrait, also 1896. A shameless celebration of his own lips. The left eye, however, blackened by shadow, looked like it was blackened by a fist. I tried to imagine myself at fifteen. I remembered my brother teaching me to drive in the parking lot of the V.A.

Only the juvenilia interested me. I walked indifferently through the rose rooms and blue rooms and nodded to the guards; I brought them greetings from the museum guards of Madrid. If Teresa were there, I would have asked her: what painting would you most like to stand in front of hour after hour, day after day? It wasn't the same question as what is your favorite painting. Or what period would you most like to dwell in and protect. Would you prefer to have to see, month after month, the figurative or the abstract? I remembered learning to drive and bonfires at Lake Clinton and what they called "experimenting" with alcohol and drugs. A tentative procedure; an act or operation for the purpose of discovering something unknown or of testing a principle or supposition. Now I was an experimental writer.

My mom, whenever we went to a museum, told me that painting seemed to have developed in reverse; that if an alien were to arrive at a museum, the alien would think the abstract canvases came first, hundreds if not thousands of years before the Renaissance. Unless the alien happened to look like a yellow triangle abutting a plane of blue. I always dismissed this theory in my mother's presence, but if Teresa were with me, I would have offered it as my own. You could say it about Picasso's particular development and it would sound intelligent, right or wrong. In the gallery devoted to Picasso's relation to African art, there were two young kids, six or seven. I didn't see the rest of the family. One walked up quickly to a large canvas and pawed it, clearly on a dare. Both kids ran out of the gallery, presumably back to their parents. There was no guard around. I approached the canvas the child had touched, a miniature precursor of, or study for, *Les Demoiselles d'Avignon*. I double-checked no one was around and, since the world was ending, touched the painting myself.

While I was attempting to hail a cab back to El Barrio Gótico, the rain intensified. I tried to reenter the museum, but couldn't find my ticket, and the guard refused to let me pass. I crossed the street and ducked into a video-game arcade that had a few of the electronic gambling machines old men were always playing; such arcades were everywhere in Spain, but I'd never been inside one. I walked to the end of the arcade, past various flashing lights and blaring soundtracks and one or two kids, until I arrived at a car-shaped game in which I could sit down. I was dripping. I leaned my head against the wheel and felt the full force of my shame. I wasn't capable of fetching coffee in this country, let alone understanding its civil war. I hadn't even seen the Alhambra. I was a violent, bipolar, compulsive liar. I was a real American. I was never going to flatten space or shatter it. I hadn't seen *The Passenger*, a movie in which I starred. I was a pothead, maybe an alcoholic. When history came alive, I was sleeping in the Ritz. A blonde woman, if that's the word, with exaggerated breasts and exaggerated eyes, was waving a checkered flag on the screen before me. I dare you to play again, she said in English.

I left the arcade. It had stopped raining. I hailed a cab to El Barrio Gótico. When the cabdriver attempted to make small talk, I said in Spanish that I didn't speak Spanish. He said one or two things to me in English and, when I didn't respond, French. When we arrived at the neighborhood's edge, I overpaid him and resumed my search. After a few minutes, I thought I saw the first café, the one I'd entered upon leaving Teresa. I went down every street radiating out from the café but could not locate the hotel. It had been how many hours? I was beginning to find it a little difficult to breathe, the prodrome of panic. I asked an elderly man what time it was; it was six or seven something, alarmingly late. I entered what might have been the same café where I'd eaten the tortilla, all the cafés were by this point interchangeable, ordered sparkling water and tried to relax. I felt like the right thing to do should have been obvious. I felt another Isabel-related pang. I longed for the Alhambra and cursed the spidery Sagrada Familia. I ordered a real drink and considered calling my parents, asking their advice, and felt embarrassed; I considered getting a hotel room, going to sleep, figuring everything out tomorrow. By the third drink, I was considering leaving not only Barcelona, but Spain altogether, and never seeing Teresa again. Were the links that tenuous?

When night was imminent the panic was upon me, a thin layer of cold foil under my skin. I took a tranquilizer. I left the café and began to walk the neighborhood again. Within three minutes of leaving the café I found myself before what was unmistakably our hotel. Only when illuminated by streetlights did I recognize the façade. My first reaction was fury, not relief; fury that it had been here all along. My fury dissipated into worry about what I would tell Teresa. The panic, at least, was gone, replaced with an almost painful sobriety. I wondered if Teresa was still there and entered the hotel to find out. The woman behind the desk looked at me significantly and picked up the phone. I ran up the stairs and knocked on the door and Teresa opened it. She turned immediately back into the room and I followed her. Her little bag was packed and on the bed.

"I have been lost all day," I said. It sounded like a lie.

"Why didn't you call me?" she asked. She was disconcertingly calm.

"I don't have your phone number," I said.

"I have given you my number many times," she said, which was true.

"I don't have it. I'm sorry. I have spent twelve hours walking around this neighborhood," I said, feeling the exhaustion.

"You walked around the neighborhood all day," she asked, as if she knew everywhere I'd been.

"And I walked down Las Ramblas to the water and I went to the Picasso museum. I thought that maybe you were there," I said.

"You went to the beach and you went to a museum," she confirmed. It did sound outrageous.

"I went to the beach to think before looking for the hotel again." I couldn't remember the Spanish expressions for "clear my head" or "gather my thoughts." "And I went to the museum because I thought you were maybe there." It didn't sound right. Of course she wouldn't have gone to the museum. "I'm sorry," I said. I wanted to defend myself but my Spanish was crumbling. Somehow switching to English would mean conceding everything.

"I have to go back to Madrid," she said flatly.

"Why?" was all I could manage.

"I'm needed at the gallery," she said. "The night train leaves in an hour or so. We should go to the station soon."

I blinked at her. "I'm not going back yet," I said to our mutual surprise.

She looked at me directly for the first time since I'd returned. "Why?"

"I might not be in Barcelona again and there is a poet here I want to see," I lied. I did not want to stay without her, but I felt it would be humiliating to return with her now like a shamed child.

She stared at me. "O.K.," she said eventually, making herself smile. "The hotel is paid for through tomorrow at five. I'll see you in Madrid." She kissed me quickly on both cheeks and left. She always left a room like someone who would be right back.

I took one of the longer showers of my project. I could not represent to myself the day I had passed; it was contentless and repetitious and thus formless; now, in the steam, it was fading. The exchange with Teresa had transpired with disorienting speed. I barely dried myself and lay down and smoked and was grateful to be too tired to ruminate for long. I thought of Levin sweating out his alienation in the fields. I thought of Picasso producing masterpieces in his sleep.

———

In post–March 11 Madrid, there was a flurry of activity at the foundation; there were several panels with minor politicians and major professors and local journalists and one or two fellows about the bombings and their political effects. I never attended, but I skimmed the e-mails. When I got back from Barcelona, there was a message from one of María José's assistants inviting me to join a panel about "literature now," a panel that would involve another fellow and a few local writers and literary critics; I didn't respond. I was still trying to formulate a way to excuse myself from the panel when, a few days after the first message, I received an e-mail from María José thanking me for agreeing to participate. The panel would be held in the foundation's auditorium on such and such evening; she looked forward to seeing me.

My terror at the prospect of the panel dovetailed with my increasing anxiety regarding what I would do when I completed my research; there were only two months of the fellowship left. I was not a sufficiently published writer to apply for jobs teaching what was called "creative writing"; Cyrus was threatening to move into his parents' basement in Topeka if things weren't repaired with Jane; whatever appeal Brooklyn held was diminished by the work I'd have to do in order to subsist there; I was determined never to set foot in Providence again. I had intended to apply to PhD programs in literature, but I knew people who'd intended to do that for years; I'd never gotten beyond bookmarking a few university home pages. The idea of law school occurred to me repeatedly, involuntarily, often with a shudder. In order not to worry about the particulars of what I would do upon my return, I framed my decision as a choice between staying and going, as if that decision had to precede, was independent of, where in particular I would go and what, in either event, I would actually do. In the final phase of my research, as the days continued to lengthen and warm, I evaluated every meal, conversation, and walk in terms of whether or not it justified or invalidated staying on. I was at once more distant and more proximal to my own experience than ever before; on the one hand, my attention was redoubled: every bite of food or phrase of overheard conversation or slant of light or corner of the museum was information for me to mull as I made my decision; on the other hand, whatever the object of my intensified attention, it was immediately abstracted into my ruminations about the future.

Arturo had said in Rafa's presence that if I stayed in Spain I could have a room at Rafa's house for as long as I liked, and Rafa had nodded his assent; the prospect of being a writer in residence in a modern palace frequented by the beautiful was not without its allure, however exhausting it would be for my face. Or, with my Ivy League degree, I could certainly find a job teaching English for corporations or rich kids; most Americans in Madrid made a living thus; they paid you under the table in cash so you didn't need a visa, and being in Spain illegally for a white American was no problem whatsoever. I didn't need to worry about health insurance, it might also have occurred to me, especially with the Socialists in power. The people I loved could come and visit. But in certain moments, I was convinced I should go home, no matter the mansion, that this life wasn't real, wasn't my own, that nearly a year of being a tourist, which is what I indubitably was, was enough, and that I needed to return to the U.S., be present for my family, and begin an earnest search for a mate, career, etc. Prolonging my stay was postponing the inevitable; I would never live away from my family and language permanently, even if I could work out the logistics, and since I knew that to be the case, I should depart at the conclusion of my fellowship, quit smoking, and renew contact with the reality of my life; that would be best for me and my poetry.

In other moments, however, the discourse of the real would seem to fall on the side of Spain; *this,* I would say to myself, referring to the hemic taste of chorizo or the aromatic spliff or both of those things on Teresa's breath, *this* is experience, not because things in Iberia were inherently more immediate, but because the landscape and my relation to it had not been entirely standardized. There would of course come a point when I would be familiar enough with the language and terrain that it would lose its unfamiliar aspect, a point at which I would no longer see a stone in Spain and think of it as, in some essential sense, *stonier* than the sedimentary rocks of Kansas, and what applied to stones applied to bodies, light, weather, whatever. But that moment of familiarization had not yet arrived; why not stay until it was imminent? Maybe if I remained I would pursue the project described so many months ago in my application, composing a long and research-driven poem, whatever that might mean, about the literary response to the Civil War, exploring what such a moment could teach us about " literature now." My Spanish would rapidly improve; I would not read Ashbery or Garnett or anything else in English, but hurl myself headlong at the Spanish canon; I would become the poet I pretended to be and realize my project. I would buy a phone and consummate my relationship with Teresa.

I was amazed to find myself protective of my poetry, comparing my options' conduciveness to writing as though obliged to do so by my genius, a genius I knew I didn't have; no duende here, I would think to myself, checking my body for sensation, no deep song. But my research had taught me that the tissue of contradictions that was my personality was itself, at best, a poem, where "poem" is understood as referring to a failure of language to be equal to the possibilities it figures; only then could my fraudulence be a project and not merely a pathology; only then could my distance from myself be redescribed as critical, aesthetic, as opposed to a side effect of what experts might call my substance problem, felicitous phrase, the origins of which lay not in my desire to evade reality, but in my desire to have a chemical excuse for reality's unavailability. But wasn't my relationship with substance also fake? I never injected anything; if I started pissing blood, I'd go to a doctor, not a bar; I planned to quit everything except social drinking, the appropriate dosage of my pills, and an occasional, whimsical smoke; I was destined to reproduce the bourgeois family, no matter how much I dreaded the prospect or wanted it postponed. Or was that the lie, the claim that my excessive self-medication was simulated; was the lie that I was in fact bound for health and respectability and so should enjoy getting fucked up while I could; had I stepped into the identity I projected, the identity of an addict; had the effort to prolong my adolescent experimentation indefinitely shaded imperceptibly into fearsome if mundane dependence, had mythomania become methomania? I less thought than felt these things on my skin as I wandered the city.

I was surprised one afternoon when I returned from El Retiro to see mail sticking out of the mailbox I almost never checked; it was a flyer for the panel. My nervousness was compounded by how serious it looked, including photos of the foundation's guests: Javier Torres, a novelist and book critic for *El País,* whose headshot made him look like a presidential candidate; Elena López Portillo, professor of literature at UCM, who looked distinguished, gray headed in front of her bookcases; Teresa Solano, translator, poet, visual artist, and curator, who was pictured squinting and smoking and engaged in conversation; and Francesc Balda, a thirty-something Catalan novelist and political journalist, handsome, also smoking, facing the camera, shaved head. Two fellows working in relevant fields would join the panel, the flyer said. I stood there looking at Teresa's picture for a long time, letting it sink in. I had not mentioned the panel to her because I was afraid she would insist on attending, but that didn't explain why she hadn't mentioned it to me; I saw her almost every day. I felt her inclusion was an act of aggression, an attack on me from María José, who wanted to humiliate me in front of Teresa; Teresa wanted to humiliate me in front of the foundation. I was furious and felt betrayed, but I was also disconcerted to discover, to be discovering so late, that Teresa had a reputation that could justify her presence in such company; according to the internet, Balda and Torres were famous, López Portillo was the world's leading authority on several Spanish poets, and then there was Teresa; why hadn't I ever Googled her before? She wasn't famous, but she had a forthcoming book of poems, her translations from Catalan and French had appeared in the major periodicals, and she had won various prizes for emerging writers. Visual artist? I knew she had published translations, but I didn't know about the forthcoming book; we had never exchanged a word about her poetry, and it somehow never occurred to me to be curious about her standing in the literary circles, whatever they were.

When I finished reading about Teresa, I set out immediately for her apartment, a thirty- or forty-minute walk from Huertas. When I had returned from Barcelona, I had feared the worst, that Teresa was through with me, and for the first couple of days I could not find her at her apartment or the gallery. Finally she came by my apartment with new drafts of her translations; she betrayed no anger or irritation or newly established distance. Now that it was heating up, she was wearing a tank top and I could see her dark shoulders and the back I'd wept down. I apologized again for getting lost and told her how embarrassing the whole thing was. She said she had been worried and irritated but insisted, largely with her smile, that it was no big deal. When she asked me what poet I met up with, I gave her a name I had found on the internet and was relieved when she said she'd never heard of him. I said it was an awkward, boring conversation, and that I wished I'd returned with her. In fact I had awoken early and taken the first train back to Madrid. From that time on I saw Teresa almost every afternoon and often spent the night at her apartment; while we continued to kiss and fool around, we did not make love. This struck me as strange, but not worrisome; maybe I liked protecting the idea of our making love from clumsy attempts at its actualization. I told myself that we were taking it slow, that our connection to one another was so ardent, it had to be managed with extreme care; maybe Teresa was waiting to hear that I would stay in Spain before giving herself more fully to our relationship. That she made out with or maybe fucked Carlos and various other pretty boys, while filling me with jealous rage, only supported my theory of our exceptionality; if she didn't find me attractive, she would have long since stopped seeing me; and if she did find me attractive, why would such a physically uninhibited person decline to sleep with me? Only, I reasoned, because she was shielding herself from the intensity of her own emotions. But now the panel somehow cast all this in doubt. As I cut through Chueca and passed near the site of our first meeting, I began to suspect she was merely toying with me, that for whatever reason, maybe because she thought I had seen Isabel in Barcelona, she was going to reveal to the foundation and her distinguished peers that I was, at best, a charlatan.

By the time I reached her building, I was hot and thirsty and indignant. Some kind of courier, cardboard tube tucked under his arm, was leaving the building when I arrived, so I didn't ring the bell. The elevator did not require the key and when the doors opened, I did not see her. Then I heard the shower. I drank a glass of water, poured myself a real drink, and sat down on her couch. I was glad she would be shocked to see me, maybe scream; I was shocked to see her on the flyer. Fuck you, I said to the cat, who was blinking its knowing blink.

She wasn't shocked. She emerged wrapped in a towel, saw me, approached and kissed me, then walked to her closet to select her clothes.

"We're on the panel together," I said flatly, watching the action of her shoulders as she searched through her wardrobe.

"Yes," she said.

"Why didn't you tell me?" I asked, attempting to betray no anger.

"I thought you knew. María José told me you were on the panel and I assumed you were the one who asked her to invite me." I was reluctant to admit it was reasonable.

"I'm not going to do it," I said.

"Why?" she asked, but didn't seem particularly to care.

"Because I have nothing to say. Because I don't speak good Spanish. Because literature isn't politics." My intensity was misplaced.

She pulled on jeans and a white tank top, which made her skin appear darker. She sat down beside me. "I have known you for six or seven months," she said, almost sadly. "We only speak Spanish. When are you going to admit that you can live in this language?" she asked.

I was touched by this, mainly because I thought she was inviting me to live in Spanish with her, to stay beyond the fellowship. My anger dissipated. "I can live in this language with you, but not with María José and the foundation. Besides, I have nothing to say about 'literature now,'" I said.

Again there was something like sadness: "Adam, you are a wonderful poet, a serious poet. If I weren't sure about that, why would I be translating you? When are you going to stop pretending that you're only pretending to be a poet?" She said only my name in English.

"You project what you pretend to discover in my poetry," I said in English.

She took my cigarette from me and I lit another. "No," she said simply, whether in English or Spanish I couldn't tell.

We sat in silence and I wondered if Teresa was right; was I in fact a conversationally fluent Spanish speaker and a real poet, whatever that meant? It was true that when I spoke to her in Spanish I was not translating, I was not thinking my thoughts in English first, but I was nevertheless outside the language I was speaking, building simple sentences with the blocks I'd memorized, not communicating through a fluid medium. But why didn't I just suck it up, attend the panel, and share my thoughts in my second language without irony? They wanted the input of a young American poet writing and reading abroad and wasn't that what I was, not just what I was pretending to be? Maybe only my fraudulence was fraudulent. Regardless, Teresa's presence would protect me, not humiliate me;

that she had selected my work to translate would lend it prestige, underwrite it, so to speak, and she would intervene if I talked myself into a corner at any point. I would be nervous and maybe it would be awkward but it would not be disastrous; María José would be placated, and my relation to Teresa would be publicized, helping to establish us in our own minds as a couple. I could send a copy of the fancy flyer to my mother. I leaned over and kissed her; she smelled like smoke and, because of the soap, lavender.

"I'm not going back to the United States," I heard myself say.

Her eyes widened and I thought her smile diminished. "Really?"

"I mean I'm not going back in June," I said. "I will probably go back eventually," I said. I was waiting for her to be excited.

"Good," she said, but my stomach sank at her lack of emotion. Or was it my heart.

"I'll write and teach English and travel," I said to say something.

"Good," she repeated, with more, but insufficient, emotion, as the smile returned fully to her face. "You can come with me to Córdoba in June and meet my family," she said. I was reassured; she was thinking long term. She did not, however, seem to be thinking of the long term with excitement.

"I would like to," I said, careful not to sound excited myself. "And I would like to spend more time in Barcelona," I said, inviting her with my eyebrows to consider whether Isabel or another woman might be awaiting me there. "And to go back to Granada," I added, to make sure Isabel was evoked. "I never saw the Alhambra."

"You went to Granada but didn't see the Alhambra," she confirmed, squinting.

"Yes," I said. I hoped she thought I was too busy making passionate love to Isabel to see the sights. "Arturo and Rafa said I could stay at Rafa's," I said, and stared at her hard, gauging her response.

"Yes, I know," she said, implying they had discussed it, but not revealing which side of the discussion she was on.

"But I'll probably just keep my apartment," I said.

"Yes, stay in the city," she said. Then, "Stay here, where I am." Now she sounded excited. She kissed me with unusual intensity and boundless, if blurry, prospects opened up.

Only an hour or two later, when we were leaving the apartment to get dinner, did the fact that I did not in reality know if I was staying in Madrid begin to bother me, and the fact that it took so long for it to bother me also began to bother me. What would Teresa say if I told her I had changed my mind, that I had decided, after all, to return to the States? As we walked back into Chueca, the plaza bustling now in late spring weather, and stood in line for a table at the restaurant, Bazaar, I decided I didn't care what she'd think; all of this, all of Spain, would cease to be real if I went back; it would be my year abroad, a year cast out of the line of years, a last or nearly last hurrah of juvenility, but it would not, in any serious sense, form part of my life. I would not stay in touch with Teresa or Arturo, not to mention Isabel; I would compose a one- or two-sentence summary of my time in Spain for those who queried me about my experience abroad, but I would otherwise recall a blur of hash and sun and maybe that kid with blood streaming down his face; everything else would be excised. If this didn't strike me as a ruthless or stupid way to think, that was because I could not believe Teresa would ultimately mind; we would have the chapbook as a memento and she would begin her next project, thinking of me no more and probably less than she thought of Carlos, Abel, whoever that guy was at Rafa's party, et al. Eventually we were seated, ate things draped in various oils, drank two or three bottles of dry cava, and discussed Gaudí, Topeka, Lorca, New York, Córdoba, Orson Welles. I believed I contributed intelligent things, speaking and understanding effortlessly. We were drunk by the time we finished dinner and as we wound our way back to her apartment I thought to myself, this is wonderful, the life I lead here, no matter if it's mine.

The two days I spent before the panel, however, were not wonderful, were definitely my own; a low-level but constant panic had come upon me; I couldn't stop grinding my teeth. Maybe I could just be silent, not say a single word, but use my face to modulate my silence and let that be my contribution; surely the more distinguished panelists would hold forth, hold court. I didn't answer the buzzer and I didn't leave the apartment. I wrote out a few sentences of wide applicability with the help of my dictionary and attempted to commit them to memory: "No writer is free to renounce his political moment, but literature reflects politics more than it affects it, an important distinction." I searched the internet for short quotes from Ortega y Gasset, who I had at one time thought was two people, like Deleuze and Guattari, Calvin and Hobbes. I figured out how to say: "I'm hesitant to speak about the Spanish condition as if I were an expert; to do so would be to fulfill the stereotypes regarding American presumptuousness." Each time I mangled a quote, I grew more nervous. I was less concerned about exposing my ignorance of Spanish poetry than I was about exposing my ignorance of Spanish *period*. I might be able to produce several grammatically perfect sentences on the cuff, or is it off, but I might not; better to mimic spontaneous if oblique pronouncements than to rely on real-time fluency.

On the day of the panel I left the apartment almost two hours early. I walked to the foundation's building, which was not far from Teresa's, then circled the block, practicing my memorized passages, reminding myself to breathe. I had three tranquilizers in the pocket of my jeans. I put my hand in my pocket to confirm their presence and contact with the denim made me exclaim internally: Why, in the name of God, was I wearing jeans? And worse: a T-shirt. In two days of panicky anticipation I had failed to concern myself with my appearance. I felt nauseated as I imagined the men in suits, María José and the professor in pantsuits; Teresa would appear elegant in whatever she wore. I asked a man at a kiosk for the time; I had a little more than an hour; if I hurried, nearly ran, I could make it. I was telling myself it was a terrible idea to get sweaty and risk being late, but I was telling myself this as I rushed back to my apartment, flew up the stairs, and looked for my suit. Thankfully, and uncharacteristically, I had hung it up after the single time I wore it, and if it wasn't pressed, it was nevertheless passable. I changed as quickly as I could, checked myself in the mirror, and flew back down the stairs. I slowed down a block from the foundation, wiped the sweat from my face, and tried to catch my breath.

I entered the building and made my way to the auditorium; to my horror, it was considerably larger than I expected, seating perhaps two hundred people, and it was full; I had anticipated a glorified conference room. I saw someone setting up a video camera on a tripod. There was a little stage, and on the stage a table with chairs, placards, a swan-shaped jug of water, glasses, and individual microphones; the stage was intensely illuminated. Four of the six panelists, including Teresa, were already seated, chatting with one another. I hesitated near the door, a little dazed; María José saw me, approached, and said, perhaps sarcastically, that I looked very elegant, then asked me to take my seat. The other fellow, she told me as she walked me toward the stage, was not able to join us. She arranged this, I told myself, enraged; as the only American, I would have to speak and the panelists or audience members would, if only out of politeness, ask me for my "perspective." I took my place at the table and received

Teresa's smile; she looked no less comfortable on stage than in her living room, although she was wearing some kind of charcoal ensemble that made me glad I'd changed clothes. I tried to smile back and saw the other panelists had pens and paper, presumably to take notes, whereas I had brought nothing, a sign of presumptuousness.

A movie I had never seen.

Soon María José ascended the stage. The crowd quieted down as she walked to a standing microphone I had not seen. She thanked everyone for coming to tonight's discussion. She then proceeded to introduce the panelists, noting, when she got to me, that a bilingual selection of my poems was shortly forthcoming, and she said we would begin the evening by asking each of the panelists to speak informally for one or two minutes about the topic, "literature now." We would begin with Javier Torres, who was seated on the end of the table nearest María José, and work our way across; I was second from last.

Again the anger rose inside me; surely María José had told the other panelists to prepare a few minutes of remarks, but had somehow neglected to say as much to me. But as Javier Torres began to speak in his politician's voice, a voice that fit his headshot perfectly, a voice that sounded like it came not from a body but a screen, my anger was nothing compared to my anxiety; I had no idea what to say. I reached into my pocket for my tranquilizers and realized, no doubt blanching, that I had failed to transfer them to my suit pants from my jeans. I felt a surge of terror so intense I was dizzy; it was like I was looking down into the space between the winding stairs of the Sagrada Familia, a view I'd never seen. Somehow Teresa, next after Javier, was already speaking; soon it would be my turn. The audience was invisible from the stage because of the lights but I could sense its presence, its attentiveness; Teresa made a joke and they laughed and the many-headed laughter was terrible to me. Elena López Portillo was talking now; I wiped the sweat from my brow. If I'd brought paper, I managed to think, I could have composed something coherent. Use your memorized lines, I told myself, but could not remember them. I was going to flee or vomit or faint.

But a line materialized. Elena López Portillo had ceased to speak and I could feel a change in pressure on my face, the effect of the audience focusing its eyes upon me. I heard myself say, my voice sounding to me as though it issued from the back of the auditorium, from deep within the audience itself, "Ortega y Gasset wrote 'By speaking, by thinking, we undertake to clarify things, and that forces us to exacerbate them, dislocate them, schematize them. Every concept is in itself an exaggeration.'" I paused, and could feel the silence tighten, as the audience attempted to take the quotation in. I was encouraged enough by my own prefabricated fluency and by the fact that I did not sound nervous or crazy, to add: "My fear about this panel is that we are in a hurry to define a period, to speak of litera-ture *now;* every period, like every concept, is in itself an exaggeration. I hope to hear from others what changed on March 11 that permits we to speak," my grammar faltered, but I could see the sentence's end, "of a new *now,* of a new period, without dislocation." I stopped there, making my brevity seem the issue of my pithiness and courage, the courage to contest the concept of the panel, when in fact I didn't want to use up any more of my quotations. A murmur of interest ran through the crowd; a current of adrenaline coursed through my body. I glanced at Teresa as Francesc Balda began to speak and I thought her smile communicated pride in me. Now I could attempt to listen to the other panelists; Francesc Balda began by stressing the importance of my point; he shared my healthy suspicion of neat distinctions between a pre-this and a post-that; indeed, perhaps literature's role was to help us keep our perspective, to take the long view, to allow us to link our "now" to various past "nows" in order to form an illuminating constellation. He then went on to describe something about Catalan literature and its relation to political violence that I failed to follow.

After our brief remarks, María José thanked us and said we'd now take questions from the audience, that microphones were in the aisles, if needed. The house lights were raised a little. The first questions were for particular panelists, but not for me, and I felt increasingly confident that I would be required to speak very little for the remainder of the panel. Someone asked Teresa how she thought her perspective on the relationship between politics and art differed from, say, Elena's because she had never experienced Franco, being born so near his death, and at some point during her answer, she said something about everyone reflecting his or her historical moment. In a burst of bravado I leaned into my microphone and added: "I agree. No writer is free to renounce his political moment, but literature reflects politics more than it affects it, an important distinction." Again the murmur, whether of agreement or disagreement, I couldn't tell, but certainly no one suspected me of being a monolingual fraud; it was a respectable point made well.

But it was stupid to have talked; now Elena, distinguished professor, directed a question at me: "Then why write at all?" She said it without malice, but I was unequivocally the addressee, and I was now required to respond, and against the backdrop of my memorized quip, my speech would seem all the more halting and confused. Any answer would do, cryptic or funny, but I was unable to locate my Spanish; time was passing and I'd parted my lips, but I could not formulate any response. Finally, I said: "I don't know." Luckily, Javier took this up as a serious answer, offering a cliché about the art choosing the artist as much as the artist chooses the art. I would not repeat, I promised myself, the mistake of speaking unless forced to speak. The panel continued and there was a long exchange with Francesc about a Catalan writer I'd never heard of, and a skirmish with Javier about *El País's* coverage of some political affair. There were multiple questions for Teresa about her participation in the protests, the possibility of literature as protest, and so on, but I had trouble comprehending her answers. Whenever my fear decreased, a profound fatigue, a fatigue that made concentration as impossible as the fear, broke over me. It was when I was emerging from a spell of fatigue that I realized a question had been addressed to me.

"Can you repeat the question, please?" I asked.

"What Spanish poets have had the greatest influence on your writing and your thinking about the relationship between poetry and political events?" was more or less what I thought he said.

To avoid a long period of silence resulting in another "I don't know," I threw him a quotation barely related to his question, if at all: "I'm hesitant to speak," I said, "about Spanish literature as if I were an expert; to do so would be to fulfill the stereotypes regarding American presumptuousness." Why it was presumptuous to list Spanish poets I admired was anybody's guess.

"But who are the poets who have influenced you personally?" the man repeated. This question, perhaps offered out of sympathy for how few queries had been addressed to me, could not have been easier to answer. Just list a few names. "Lorca," I lied. "Miguel Hernández." But then, to my horror and amazement, I could not think of another poet; my head was emptied of every Spanish proper name; I couldn't even think of common names to offer as though they were little known authors. Forget annotating the list, explaining how one poet's sense of line or of the social influenced my own poetic practice, or relating these poets to my previous comments: just list a few fucking names. Finally I thought of two famous poets I'd barely read: Juan Ramón Jiménez and Antonio Machado, but the names collided and recombined in my head, and I heard myself say: "Ramón Machado Jiménez," which was as absurd as saying "Whitman Dickinson Walt," and a few people tittered. I corrected myself, but it came out wrong again: "Antonio Ramon Jimenez," and now those who were baffled understood my unforgivable error, so extreme they might have at first suspected it was an ironic gesture; several people laughed. The celebrated American fellow cannot get four names deep into the list of the most famous Spanish poets of the twentieth century. "Jiménez and Machado," I finally said, at least separating the poets out, but it was too late; I had embarrassed myself, the foundation, and I had ruined everything with Teresa. María José said we would take only one more question because of time, but surely she meant because of shame, because of the great shame the foundation felt at sponsoring an American phony, although she was no doubt personally delighted with the scene.

When I confirmed the last question wasn't for me, I didn't listen; I just counted the seconds until María José thanked us and asked the crowd to applaud, made some announcement about another panel, asked the crowd to applaud again, and then the lights were fully on and the audience slowly began to leave its seats. Before I could flee,

Teresa was upon me, smiling as if nothing had happened, assuring me I had done wonderfully, then chatting with the other panelists. I sat there and said to myself: You'll be gone in six weeks. You will never see any of these people again. María José cannot nullify your fellowship because you mangled names. None of this matters. Not Teresa or the panel or Spain or Spanish literature or literature in general. Now María José was thanking each of the panelists in turn; she reached me and said my contributions had been brilliant. I smiled a mirthless smile that communicated infinite disdain and thanked her. To myself I was saying: You don't love Teresa and she doesn't love you. None of this is real. You don't like Madrid, with its tourists and dust and heat and innumerable Pietàs and terrible food. The fucking fascists. You are ready to quit smoking, to clean up, to return to friends and family. You have outgrown poetry. You will be a legitimate scholar or a lawyer but you are done with Teresa and hash and drinking and lying and lyric and the intersections thereof. I have never been here, I said to myself. You have never seen me.

———

In the last phase of my research fireflies were disappearing. Bats were flying around confused in the middle of the day, colliding with each other, falling into little heaps. Bees were disappearing, maybe because of cell phone radiation, maybe because of perfume, maybe because of candy. It was the deadliest day since the invasion began. Unmanned drones made sorrowful noise overhead. It was 1933. The cities were polluted with light, the world warming. The seas were rising. The seas were closing over future readers. Confused trees were blooming early; you could view the pics from space online. It was 1066, 312. Why not let the children touch the paintings? You could see the hooded prisoners in orange jumpsuits behind the concertina wire. I was standing before *The Descent,* oil on oak, hash and caffeine; I hadn't been there in a while and the blue was startling. 1936, 1492, 800, 1776. Meanwhile, life's white machine. The great artist and the museum guard. Having nothing to say and saying it into a tiny phone. ¿Por qué nací entre espejos? I wondered if the guard in the Reina Sofía ever wore her necklace. Before the reading, I had a couple of hours to kill. Bajo el agua / siguen las palabras. I left the museum for the park.

It was a beautiful day, unseasonably cool, and the park was crowded; there were puppet shows and portraitists near El Estanque. The hash dealers were back, or reinforcements had arrived, milling around the trees. I found a bench and opened my chapbook; it was wonderfully made, its quality anachronistic, befitting a dead medium. Letterpressed on Italian paper, hand sewn. Arturo had printed a thousand copies. Teresa's name only appeared on the front matter, as she had insisted. Arturo had invited everybody to the reading and celebration. I'd even agreed to forward the announcement to my entire inbox, although I only knew four or five people in Spain. I was wearing my suit. I'd received an e-mail María José sent out to all the fellows informing them about the event. Come celebrate a wonderful accomplishment, etc. For whatever reason, I wasn't nervous. Maybe Elena López Portillo would attend and write an essay on my work. Maybe Isabel would bring Oscar, whom I imagined as Carlos. Teresa said her publisher was considering asking me for a book. Under the water / the words go on. I would have liked to kiss Rufina. Over the course of my research, I'd lost considerable weight. Other than that, I didn't think I'd undergone much change.

It would cost a hundred euros to change an international ticket, less than a meal at Zalacaín. The museum guard, the bathroom attendant, the economic mode. I walked to the colonnade and listened to the drummers. The sun was just beginning to set, and the light had softened, but there would be some light until nearly ten. I sat and smoked and, for whatever reason, thought: Teresa should read the originals; I'll read the translations. My accent, when I read, was good, much better, I didn't know why, than when I spoke. I sat on the colonnade and read a poem or two aloud in Spanish; I didn't hear an American accent.

I eventually made my way to the gallery, which I was pleased to see was overflowing. If I was nervous, it was only about the fact that I wasn't nervous, which might mean something was wrong with me. I was greeted by various people: María José was surprisingly warm; we kissed each other without irony. One of the swimmers I had smoked with caught the corner of my mouth. I found Teresa, who looked stunning, and we kissed each other on the lips. She was wearing a dress that was probably satin, silver, very simple, but unmistakably expensive. We didn't know many working people. I told her about my idea, that we'd swap parts in the reading, and although there were trace amounts of sadness in her smile, she agreed.

There was a bar and, to my surprise, a bartender. I asked him for white wine. While he was pouring my wine, Jorge approached me; he must have been in my inbox. We embraced each other warmly. He said something about how far my Spanish had come, about the fancy people I'd fallen in with, how he'd tell people in the future all about the famous poet he tutored and sold drugs to. I asked him if he could name a famous living poet. He couldn't.

"Is Isabel back in Madrid?" I asked him.

"What do you mean?" he said.

"Is she back from Barcelona?" I asked.

"When did she go to Barcelona?" he asked, puzzled.

"Is she working at the language school again?" I asked.

"She never stopped working at the language school," he said.

"Oh," I said. I waited for an emotional reaction to this news, to be thrilled or angry or at least suspicious. Had she made up the Oscar story? Had she changed her mind? Had he come early? I waited, but only felt a little curious; I was otherwise unmoved. I wondered if she was in the crowd. I wondered again if there were something wrong with me.

There was a table with stacks of the chapbook for sale; it was strange to see so many copies of my name. They cost ten euros, which seemed like a lot. Arturo came up to me and hugged me and I thanked him for everything. You can make it up to me, he said, by sweeping the floors of the gallery in the coming months. He said we were about to begin and that I should sit in the front with Teresa, which I did. People stopped talking and those that couldn't find seats sat on the floor or stood in the back. I was a little nervous now, but not unpleasantly so; I thought about my tranquilizers in my suit jacket pocket only because I was surprised not to want one. Arturo appeared at the podium and began to speak. Night-blooming flowers refused to open near the stadium lights. Freedom was on the march. Aircraft noise was having strange effects on finches. Some species synchronized their flashes, sometimes across thousands of insects, exacerbating contradictions. Why was I born between mirrors?

Teresa would read the originals and I would read the translations and the translations would become the originals as we read. Then I planned to live forever in a skylit room surrounded by my friends.

ACKNOWLEDGMENTS

Thank you: Ariana, Mom, Dad, Matt, Aaron, Anna, Brecht, C. D., Chris, Colin, Cyrus, Forrest, Geoffrey, Jacqueline, Jeff, Joanna, Jo-Lynne, Justin, Kyle, Laura, Skoog, Stephen, Tao, and Tom. I have stolen language and ideas from Michael Clune's essay, "Theory of Prose," which appeared in *No: a journal of the arts*, #7. Like Clune, I am indebted to Allen Grossman's essays in *The Long Schoolroom*. I first encountered the phrase "life's white machine" in Jeff Clark and Geoffrey G. O'Brien's collaboration, *2A*. John Ashbery used the phrase as an epigraph to the poem "Longing of the Accords" (*Planisphere*). An excerpt of this book was published as a pamphlet by Physiocrats Press. The novel includes, albeit in altered form, a reading of Ashbery's poetry that first appeared in my essay "The Future Continuous: Ashbery's Lyric Mediacy," published by *boundary 2*. "Leaving the Atocha Station" is the title of a poem in Ashbery's 1962 volume *The Tennis Court Oath*.

CREDITS

Page 11: Detail of *The Descent from the Cross,* by Rogier van der Weyden (ca. 1435).

Page 52: Photo of the bombing of Guernica, 1937. Reprinted from the German Federal Archives (Deutsches Bundesarchiv).

Page 90: "Clepsydra" from *Rivers and Mountains,* by John Ashbery. Reprinted by permission of George Borchardt, Inc., on behalf of the author.

Page 103: *The Alhambra,* by Esther Singleton — Original from *Turrets, Towers, and Temples: The Great Buildings of the World, as Seen and Described by Famous Writers,* by Esther Singleton (NY: Dodd, Mead and Company, 1898). Reproduction by Liam Quin (http://www.fromoldbooks.org).

Page 141: *Francisco Franco,* 1958 is used by permission of Ramón Masats, copyright © Ramón Masats, 1958.

Page 173: Detail of a production still from *The Passenger* (1975).